WAVES

WITHDRAWN

WAVES

JARED A. CARNIE

urbanepublications.com

First published in Great Britain in 2016 by Urbane Publications Ltd
Suite 3, Brown Europe House, 33/34 Gleaming Wood Drive, Chatham, Kent ME5 8RZ
Copyright © Jared A.Carnie, 2016

A CIP catalogue record for this book is available from the British Library.

ISBN 978-1-911129-42-4
EPUB 978-1-911129-43-1
MOBI 978-1-911129-44-8

Design and Typeset by Julie Martin
Cover by Julie Martin

urbanepublications.com

The publisher supports the Forest Stewardship Council® (FSC®), the leading international forest-certification
organisation. This book is made from acid-free paper from an FSC®-certified provider. FSC is the only
forest-certification scheme supported by the leading environmental organisations, including Greenpeace.

FOR FAYE

CHAPTER 1

IT DID LOOK NICE. I wasn't going to admit it though. That's not how moping works. I was heartbroken and determined to make sure my every movement made it as obvious as possible. I tried to counter the view by putting Joy Division on.

"Jesus, Alex. Not again. I've told you. It's not like I don't like them, it's just not very road trip, is it? Neal Cassady wouldn't have put this on."

"Neal Cassady didn't feel like I feel."

"Oh fuck off."

I heard myself as James was hearing me. I laughed, apologised and put The Stooges on.

"That's better." he said.

We'd just passed a sign telling us there were no more places to stop before Ullapool. This meant James would be driving the rest of the way. We'd been swapping every few hours for the last fourteen or so. Whenever one of us got tired or needed a piss or some food we'd pull into the nearest services, swap seats and get back on the road. We had an unspoken agreement that neither of us would fall asleep at any point. We were running on Red Bull and Haribo. The steering wheel was sticky with sweat and sugar.

I watched the colours out the window. It wasn't what I'd expected from Scotland in October. There were these rich purples and greens. The sky was a clean blue. Neither of us spoke for those last forty minutes. We watched the landscape become more and more striking while Iggy taught us about Raw Power.

I'd never been through that bit of Scotland before. James hadn't either. He'd only ever flown up. He'd always wanted to do the drive but hadn't fancied it on his own.

~~~~~

When James went off to university his parents moved up to the Isle of Lewis. His mum, Mary, was born there. She'd moved down to the mainland after she met James' dad. Once he'd retired and James was out of the house they'd decided to head back North for a more peaceful life. For Mary it was a chance to be surrounded by her family again. Most of them had never left the island.

Each summer James would fly up to see them for a week or two. Whenever he told me about it he always said it was weird but spectacular. To me it just sounded like the place Father Ted lived. I'd never felt the need to visit.

That's not to say that I didn't like James' parents. I loved them. When I was a kid I used to see them all the time. We lived on the same street. They'd always give me dinner if I was playing football with James in their garden.

Mary used to call me the shoe-breaker. We must have been seven or eight when it started. James came into school wearing these new shoes. They had a leather flap over the laces. I tugged on it for some reason and it came straight off. From then on Mary always acted like I was this brute who didn't know my own strength. I pretended to still be embarrassed about it. Really I liked that she remembered. Mary was funny and never anything but kind to me.

All through school I stayed close to them. I think they appreciated me always being around as James didn't have any brothers or sisters. I didn't either. I think that's why my mum was happy to let me spend so much time at their house too.

When James went off to university they moved pretty much straight away. I was staying at home. I knew it was coming but it still hit me pretty hard. The whole street felt different. The whole town felt different.

James had gone to Bristol. His parents were up in god knows where. Some family I didn't know had moved into their old house. And Kim was all the way up in Manchester. I felt isolated. For some reason everything my mum did that used to seem caring suddenly became incredibly irritating. It just drilled into me the fact that I was stuck at home.

I knew it'd be worth it though. Mum wasn't asking for too much help with the bills and I was working and trying to save up for Kim and me. It was all for Kim. For our life together.

We'd come to a stop at Ullapool.

"You're quiet, Alex. What're you thinking about? Puppies? Rainbows?"

"Something like that, yeah."

"I think we just wait now until they wave us on. I don't think that's for a while though. I didn't see the ferry in the harbour. Did you?"

"I don't think so."

"You hungry?"

"Not sure really."

"I'm starving. Let's go get some fish and chips or something. It's better than sitting here anyway. We'll be back in time easy."

We left the car and walked down the street. It was silent. I looked out over the water. It was a little breathtaking. The hills looked like they'd been scribbled on the horizon by giggling children.

The town was barely a town at all. It was just a couple of streets. It did have a Boots. That was something, I guess. I couldn't work out whether anyone really lived there or if Ullapool was just a cluster of B&Bs and pubs waiting for whenever the ferry got cancelled and passengers were stranded, suddenly in need of shelter and alcohol.

We stopped in at a fish and chip place. The sign had drawn James in. It said they'd been voted best fish and chips in the country. I didn't really question it. James ordered and chatted to the woman serving us. He seemed in a good mood. When we were driving I felt like he was being over the top with his enthusiasm to try and balance out my sour mood. Seeing him now though, it dawned on me that maybe he'd genuinely just been excited. We were on the way to see his parents after all. He liked his parents.

We sat down outside on a wall near the water. I had a few of James' chips. There was something about eating them out of newspaper that made them taste better for some reason. I wasn't ready to say that out loud though. I knew the whole week was going to be a testament to James' ability to cheer me up and I didn't want to give him the satisfaction just yet.

"There's a bar on the ferry. You can get a few beers if you like," James said. "I should probably do the driving the other side. I know the way and it'll be pretty dark by the time we're there. It'll take you a while to adjust to the roads so it's probably best not to start in the dark. They're pretty ridiculous in some places."

"Yeah, I remember you saying. More sheep on the roads than cars or something. I always figured you were kidding about that."

"I was half-exaggerating."

"I don't think I'll drink on the ferry either to be honest. It's not really fair if you're not. Besides, I don't think it'll be great for my mood."

"So, you're admitting you might just be a little bit grumpy today?" James asked, smiling.

"Maybe," I said.

"Seriously Alex, I know you're feeling like shit. Ok? I know you are. You don't need to go out of your way to prove it to me every second of the day. I already know. That's a good sign though. Not wanting to drown your sorrows. I'm impressed."

"Well, I figure I'm going somewhere new – surely I'll find something to do that isn't drinking."

"You've definitely never been to Lewis before," he said.

I laughed. I tried to play it off as a cough but James wasn't fooled.

CHAPTER 2

JAMES WAS SITTING ACROSS FROM ME. It was getting dark outside but I could still see the sea tumbling onto itself through the window. James was drinking a can of coke. I had a pint of tap water from the bar. The Guinness glass made it feel like a compromise somehow.

James asked me how I was doing. I told him I never got sea sick. He knew not to press me anymore. James was good like that. He could read me even when I wasn't giving him anything to work with. It had been his idea for me to come.

~~~~~

We'd been sitting in a bar in Bristol when I told him what had happened. I'd come straight down to see him. He'd just finished his degree and was facing a few months of doing nothing until his job started in January. I knew he'd be able to put me up for a while. More importantly, I knew he'd be able to put up with me for a while.

I was just getting to the end of the story.

"Fucking hell. There and then?"

"Yeah. I guess she couldn't let me carry on and then tell me. It was just bad timing."

"Bad timing my arse. She's a twat. That's fucking terrible. No offence, but fuck her. Fuck her Alex. You don't need her."

It had taken me a while to explain it all. I didn't want to come across as melodramatic but it was by far the most dramatic and painful thing that had ever happened to me. Maybe anyone.

Kim was at Manchester studying medicine. It takes more than five years to get through that course. Towards the end of school, we'd started seeing each other and we'd always promised that once she'd finished her degree we'd move in together. That's why I was doing admin at the hospital and staying at home with my mum. I was saving up so that by the time she'd finished I'd be able to set us up nicely somewhere. I knew she'd have a lot of debt and didn't want her to worry.

It wasn't easy saving. I mean, my mum didn't ask too much for rent, but there were expenses. Every couple of weeks I'd have to pay to get the train up to Manchester. The first couple of times I drove but the petrol was still pretty expensive. Besides, all that time on my own in the car was exhausting. On the train at least I could put headphones in or sleep if I wanted. The problem was that the train cost sixty quid. It seemed worth it though. Otherwise we never would've seen each other.

When I was up I'd always try to give her the best time. Take her out for dinner. Plan things for us to do. I wanted it to be worth her while. That added up too.

I was still saving though. Whatever I had left over each

month I'd put away. It was for our future and that's what mattered.

I'd gone straight into this hospital job from school. It was only a mile down the road from where I went to school. The same bus I took to school as a kid actually passed by the hospital each morning. It didn't feel like progress. It was money though. That's what got me through the days. It was money.

The work itself wasn't exactly what I'd always wanted to do. It was just basic admin stuff. Typing the same names over and over into different places. I was surrounded by middle-aged women who would drive me insane with their inane conversation. I thought about the future a lot. The thought of living with Kim got me through. That and my other work. In the evenings I was writing a book, a mystery book. I'd grown up watching crime shows on TV, and after a while I could always guess the endings. I decided I would write a great mystery novel where nobody could guess the ending. I imagined kids at school racing to the end of the book to tell all their friends what had really happened.

One night I was sitting at my computer. I'd just finished a chapter. I was feeling pretty good and wanted to show someone what I'd done. That was always when I missed Kim the most. Every time I was in Manchester I'd bring up a flash drive with the latest chapter on and I'd read it to her. She was a good listener. She'd gasp in all the right places and always pretend she was dying to know what was going to happen next.

That evening everything clicked in my head. I knew what I had to do. It was the end of May and Kim was coming to the end of her year. She was going away to Malaga with her mates in June. Then she'd be back home in July before she went back up to Manchester in August. That was my chance. That was the time. Between Malaga and Manchester. I just wanted something to cling on to. Something to remind me of what I was working for. Something tangible. Something to show me that it wasn't all as empty as it felt. I was going to propose. That was it. We knew we were going to be together anyway. It was just a case of formalising it. To give everyone a chance to congratulate us and acknowledge our commitment to each other.

~~~~~

July. I drove over to Kim's parents' house the morning she was landing. I'd planned it perfectly. I'd saved up my wages since May. Three months was meant to be right. My mum let me off the rent for a bit after I told her the plan.

I knocked on the door and Kim's dad let me in. I had the ring in my pocket. I sat him down and let him know my intentions. I told him I was there for his permission. I told him I wanted to marry his daughter. He looked shocked. He called Kim's mum in. She sat down next to me. She told me that she'd always liked me and really hoped I found something to make me happy.

That was when the front door opened. It was Kim. I thought she wasn't due home until later. I wasn't quite ready.

She came in, looked surprised but still hugged me. Her parents went into the kitchen to fix us some drinks. Champagne I assumed. I kissed Kim on the forehead and told her I needed to talk to her. She told me she needed to talk to me too. She said she wanted to go first. That was fine. I figured my thing was the grand finale. I wonder what would've happened if we'd gone the other way around.

That was when she told me. She'd been seeing a guy up in Manchester. Steve. I'd met him at her birthday party she said. I had a vague memory. I wasn't really sure. I wasn't really paying attention. It was surreal. I felt bare. I felt exposed. She was saying things I swear I'd heard people say in movies. It wasn't my fault blah blah blah.

I drove home and climbed into bed. I tried to call James but couldn't get through. I pulled the covers up over my head and closed my eyes. A few minutes later my phone rang. It was James. I told him I wanted to come down and see him. He said any time. I grabbed my jacket and got straight in the car. I pulled up outside his house and told him I needed a drink. We went straight to a bar just down the road from his. Then I told him everything.

"Look. You need to forget all this. You need to be on your own. I don't mean alone, but on your own. Your own person. You've been too focused on her. You've forgotten how great you are. You're my mate. Alex. I like Alex. Alex on his own. I don't like Kim's boyfriend Alex."

"That's because Alex isn't Kim's boyfriend."

"You know what I meant. Look. Come up to Lewis with

me when I go. It'll be great. We'll drink. I'll show you the beaches. You can look at the stars and think about life or whatever. Just get some peace and quiet. Forget about all this."

"I don't know."

"Shit. You know what. I'm not actually going up until later in the year. They're having stuff done to the house. Since I'm free 'til January I said I'd just go up whenever it's all done. It probably won't be until October. But still. You should come. You have to."

"Yeah, maybe."

"No, not maybe. That's it. You're coming. We're agreed. We've made a plan."

When we were little I knew everything there was to know about James. I knew where he hid his favourite toys. I knew what made him cry. At that point I realised I didn't know everything about him anymore. He'd grown and I hadn't grown with him. He was still my friend though. A great friend. And right then I didn't really have much else to rely on.

CHAPTER 3

THE LAND WAS GETTING NEARER. I'd been staring out the window so long I'd zoned out. I hadn't really noticed how long we'd been moving.

It was dark so I couldn't see far. There were a few lights dotted along the front of the harbour. It looked quite pretty. As we got closer I could make out a big glass building. I could see through to the people eating on the second floor.

James and I went down to the car. He got in the driver's side. We were the second car from the front so we got off pretty quickly once the ferry stopped.

"So what's this place we're looking for called?" I asked.

"Keose. But don't bother with the road signs. They all have the Gaelic bigger than the English. By the time you realise what you're reading we'll have already passed it. I'm pretty sure I know the way from here anyway."

Within a couple of minutes, we were out of Stornoway. There weren't any more buildings. I didn't know if we'd missed a lot of the town or seen it all already. I'd only ever seen Stornoway on the weather. I'd always assumed to make the weather map you had to be a decent size.

Soon there were no streetlights either. A couple of the

bends were pretty sharp and I told James to slow down a bit. He apologised. He said he was on autopilot. We passed a petrol station at the side of the road. Aside from that there was nothing to see except for the dark silhouette of long grass and the shadows of mountains in the distance.

We whipped round a corner. I realised for a split second we'd been facing directly at a loch with no fence between the road and the water. If we'd mistimed the turn even slightly we'd have been goners. James had told me the island was covered in lochs but I hadn't really processed it. I thought maybe there'd be a few vast lakes you could see from miles away. I didn't expect them to sneak up on you. Every corner seemed to be running alongside some dark choppy water.

"Shit. That was it."

James stopped in the middle of the road. He turned the car around and took the turning we'd missed. Once we were back on track he told me that driving here was different to driving anywhere else. He said there weren't really any rules.

We drove past a few small houses down a single track road. We got to a corner and James stopped the car. He didn't even pull over; we just came to a stop.

"This is it," he said.

We left the car there on the road. There was just enough room for another car to get by.

The house looked great. It was made of stone and wider than it was tall. There were lights on in every room. I got my bag from the boot and James did the same.

He knocked on the front door. There was no answer. We

went round the side through a little gate. I noticed the gate was carved to look like the steering wheel of a ship.

"Your parents weren't ever sailors were they?"

"When we lived down in Essex? No. Not as far as I know," he laughed. "They do have a little boat now though."

I was too exhausted to work out whether my question was stupid or not. James opened the back door and we were in. It was the kitchen. There were a few people standing around. Music was playing.

"Here they are!"

"Come in, come in."

I didn't recognise any of the faces. A man in a blue fleece came over and shook James' hand. James introduced me. The man told me his name was Angus and said he lived just down the road. I didn't know where down the road meant. I nodded and said hello.

Mary came running into the kitchen. She let out a happy little squeal.

"I just went to the front door. I wondered where you were!"

"Here we are, Mum," James said.

She gave James a big hug. Then she turned to me.

"Uh-oh. Hide your shoes everyone."

I laughed. She gave me an equally big hug.

CHAPTER 4

I'D BEEN THROUGH ABOUT FIVE HUNDRED INTRODUCTIONS. Everyone was linked in ways I couldn't get my head round. This is his cousin and he lives next door to her and these two work together and so on and so on. There were so many new faces that when Martin, James' dad, came over, it took me a second to actually recognise him. I decided I'd give up trying to remember any names for the night. It was more effort than it was worth.

I was tired but happy to be there. The swift music changes were keeping me awake. It was obviously on shuffle. It would go from The Who to some Scottish tune to Oasis. When the Proclaimers came on I couldn't help but laugh.

Mary introduced James and I to Isobel. Isobel seemed different to everyone else I'd met so far. First of all, she wasn't introduced to me with a complicated family history. Second of all, she must have been the youngest person at the party by about ten years until James and I had turned up.

As soon as we'd been introduced Mary whisked James away to say hello to someone she said he absolutely had to say hello to. I was left with Isobel. She had a glass of wine in her hand. I was sticking to water. She had the same look of happiness and discomfort on her face that I'm sure I had on my mine.

"So…" I started, not sure where I was going, "how do you know…everyone?"

My brain wasn't really working. It had been a long trip. Luckily she laughed and seemed to know what I was going for.

"I work at the hospital. I've met Mary a few times there. She invited me over."

Moondance by Van Morrison came on. I knew the intro. Everyone knew the intro. There was an instant split down the room. One middle-aged couple standing in the doorway began singing to each other. Another man started moaning loudly.

"This guy, he's a right shit. Did you hear when he played here before? Got in his car straight from the airport, played his show, straight back to the airport. Didn't say hello to anyone. Didn't stop to speak to a single person. Had his back to the crowd for half the show too. He's up his own arse. Total tosspot."

The guy kept going. Nobody was really listening.

"I've heard that story about fifty times," Isobel said. "Here's a tip for you. If you're ever not sure what to talk about while you're up here, bring up Van Morrison. People love to go on about him. They act like he bombed the place."

"Thanks for that. I'll bear that in mind."

Moondance ended and When I'm Sixty-Four came on. The angry man settled down and began singing along. He thought it was hilarious to change the words to 'now I'm sixty-four'. Again, nobody paid him much attention.

Isobel was trying to tell me something but I was finding it hard to hear her over all the noise. I watched her lips move and tried to focus. I wondered if she was single. I cursed her lovely accent for making me think like that. I was on the island to forget about that stuff. To be my own person for once.

There was a short stop in the conversation where I hadn't heard what she'd said. I was obviously meant to say something but I didn't know what. The music stopped at the exact same moment. It was an agonizing half a second. Then another Beatles song started up and I said the first thing I could think of.

"So, does anyone ever call you Izzy?"

"Izzy? No, I don't think so."

"That's a shame. You could've been like Izzy Stradlin."

"Who?"

I suddenly became aware how much the name sounded like that of a pornstar.

"He was in Guns N' Roses," I said quickly.

"Oh right. I'd rather not take my nickname from a guy all the same."

"That makes sense," I said.

I was sure she was never going to talk to me again. Mary came over and apologised for interrupting. I meant it whole-heartedly when I told her it was no problem. Mary told Isobel that her lift was about to head off. She said that she'd have to get going now if she wanted a lift back into town. I shook her hand and told her it was nice to meet her.

"Are you going to the Ceilidh tomorrow?" she asked.

"The what?"

Mary jumped in.

"Yeah, we'll all be there Isobel. We'll see you there. Thanks so much for coming."

Isobel thanked Mary in return. She made her way towards the side-door, turned and smiled at me, then left.

Mary told me that James was in the other room insisting that I meet someone. She took me through to the hallway between the kitchen and the living room. A red-faced middle-aged man was sitting on a sofa. James was standing next to him.

"Alex, this is John."

I held out my hand towards the man on the sofa. He didn't take it.

"You're welcome," he said.

He was clearly drunk. Two near-empty tumblers sat by his feet. James leaned over to me and whispered.

"I've never met him before. He's convinced he knows my face. It's really funny."

Then he turned back to John.

"So, John, tell Alex here about your special lady. She works down at the Co-op right? The woman with the limp?"

"She didn't have that limp before I got to her, son."

I winced.

"That's not what I heard," said James.

"It's the god's honest truth. You know me, son. Nothing

but the best for old John."

Back in the USSR came on. John tilted his head back onto the top of the sofa and stuck both his arms in the air. His eyes were now closed. He gargled out a few wrong lyrics through the verses. When the chorus arrived he opened his eyes and yelled along. That seemed to tire him out. After the chorus his arms fell down onto his lap and he closed his eyes again.

James and I went back to the kitchen. It seemed that most people were leaving or had already left. I saw the dock and the speakers on the kitchen windowsill. Ob-la-di, ob-la-da was playing. I knew what was happening now. I'd made the same mistake before. Someone had got so excited hearing the Beatles that they'd gone and put The White Album on shuffle. It always seems like a great idea until one of the bonkers bits comes on uninvited and you have to rush to change the track. I was worried Revolution 9 might be next. That was never good. I went and put on the Stones. Sticky Fingers. Brown Sugar. I heard a cheer from somewhere else in the house.

Mary was waving goodbye to someone from the kitchen door.

"Is there anything useful I can do, Mary?" I asked.

"No, no, Alex. Thanks very much though. Just let me know if you need anything. Oh, has James shown you where you're sleeping yet?"

I shook my head.

"Honestly. My son. No kind of host at all."

"I don't actually live here, Mum," James said.

James took me upstairs. First he showed me where he was

sleeping. It was a single bed. He said I was welcome to share that with him. I wasn't against the idea. We'd shared a bed hundreds of times. He said there was another option though.

He took me along the corridor and up another small staircase. It was the attic. Converted. Very cosy. The roof slanted down which made the room feel smaller than it was. The pitch black of the skylight wasn't much use at this hour. I turned on the light.

"Or you can just take this sofa here. It folds out I think. I know it doesn't look much but Mum said it's the quietest room in the house. My folks get up so early that I thought you might appreciate that. I'm sure some days they'll be waking me up early to go do something with them and this way you can get a bit of a lie-in. Sleep off those water hangovers."

"I'll take it," I said.

We went back downstairs. Martin was sitting on a chair by the kitchen table. Dead Flowers was playing. Martin was tapping his foot to the music. The table was covered in glasses and beer cans and wine bottles and plastic cups. There didn't seem to be anyone else left now.

I picked up a few glasses and took them over to the sink. Mary came in from the garden and ordered me to put them down. She turned the speakers off and told me to push whatever I was thinking of doing out of my head and go to bed. I thanked her, gave her a hug and headed upstairs.

When I turned the lights out I could see a few stars through the skylight. I felt exhausted but I wasn't desperate to sleep.

The house felt oddly silent. Music had been playing from the moment I arrived. I thought about turning the light back on and reading. I'd brought a few books with me. Dharma Bums. The Panopticon. Norwegian Wood. I couldn't work out whether I wanted to read anything.

I heard a stumble and a "fuck" from down the corridor. James was drunk in the dark and trying to find the toilet in a bathroom that had been completely redecorated since he was last in it.

I heard the toilet flush and his footsteps back down the corridor. Then it was silent again.

All that water was catching up with me. I desperately needed a piss but didn't want to get up. I felt at peace and didn't want to break the spell. I tried to over-rule my bladder. I kept my eyes open and stared at the sky above me. It was too dark to make anything out but I found that kind of comforting somehow.

At one point I heard some geese fly over the house. It sounded odd. I couldn't work out whether it was unusual for geese to fly so close or whether usually there was so much other noise outside I was never able to hear them.

CHAPTER 5

I WOKE UP THE NEXT MORNING FEELING PRETTY GOOD. I thought I'd spent most of the night staring up at the darkness, but by the time it was light I felt pretty refreshed so I must have fallen asleep at some point.

I slipped on my jeans and wandered over to the bathroom. In the light I had none of the problems James had had the night before. I took a long piss and felt relieved to not be hungover. Waking up in a new place hungover was always the worst. Besides, if I'd been drinking alcohol and refused to go for a piss in the night, I'd have no doubt woken up with a suspicious wet patch on the front of my boxers. A few hazy mornings I'd had to try and convince myself it was definitely something I didn't remember spilling the night before. As it was, I woke up with dry boxers and managed to make it all the way to the toilet before letting my bladder empty itself. A good start to the day.

Back in my room I could hear activity downstairs. I slipped on a t-shirt and wandered down. Mary was in the kitchen. Pots were on the hob and something was in the oven.

"How did you sleep, dear?" she asked.

"Good thanks."

"James and Martin are out the back. There's towels in the bathroom if you fancy a shower or bath. Lunch won't be for a while yet."

"Thanks, Mary."

I stood naked in the bathroom. I double-checked the door was locked. I looked at my body in the mirror. Arms raised, stomach in, it didn't look too bad. Taut enough to not be embarrassed by. As long as I didn't turn sideways. That was where the shame came from. I rotated in front of the mirror, trying to work out from which angles I looked the most manly. My body felt worn out in a satisfying way. The warmth of the shower woke my muscles up a bit. I towelled myself off and went back to my room. The skylight was now a bright blue colour.

There was a shelf full of DVDs I hadn't noticed the night before. It ran along the length of the wall. There were a lot of box sets. Sopranos. 24. Battlestar Galactica. I hadn't seen most of them. Kim and I had been watching an episode of Prison Break every time I went up to visit her, but as the series got more and more ridiculous we ended up giving up. Kim said she had so little free time she couldn't afford to waste any watching TV with me anyway. I didn't mind. I hadn't really liked the show from the start.

I took the books I'd brought with me out of my bag and put them on top of the shelf. None of them seemed the right thing to read at that moment.

Downstairs in the kitchen Mary was still hard at work.

"Get the shower working ok?" she asked. "It's a bit temperamental sometimes."

"Yeah, it was fine thanks. I wasn't actually drinking last night so it felt good to have no hangover to wash away."

"That's very sensible, Alex. I wish my boy would take a leaf out of your book. He looked like death this morning when his father took him out."

There were footsteps outside the backdoor. The door opened and a black and white collie came charging in. He ran up to me and stood up on his hind legs. I stroked around his ears. I heard Martin shout "Rupert!" from outside.

Rupert turned around and ran back outside. Then Martin came in. He was wearing clothes that nobody I knew owned. They were practical and only practical. People in Essex wouldn't be seen dead in them.

"Sorry about Rupert," Martin said. "He's got too much energy. He's been like that all morning."

"That's alright. He seemed friendly," I said.

"That's one word for it."

James came in. He was wearing the same clothes as Martin.

"Alright Alex? How you feeling?"

"Not too bad. How about you?"

"Oh, you know, nothing beats a nice bit of manual labour in the morning. Especially hungover."

I laughed. Mary turned around and eyed them both.

"Right, boys of mine, lunch will be in ten minutes so go and get cleaned up. We have company so do try and look a bit more presentable."

They followed their orders without questions.

"Can I help at all Mary?" I asked.

"Of course you can, dear. You can take a seat and let me get you a drink. There's some beers in the fridge if you'd like one. Or we've got some lemonade. Or orange juice. Or just water."

"Orange juice would be great, thanks," I said.

Mary walked over to the fridge and grabbed the orange juice carton.

"I won't mention it again Alex, but I just wanted to say, James mentioned what happened before you came up. I'm not going to pity you as I know that's the last thing you need, but I want you to know we're all here for you. I really hope you're not feeling too down. Especially up here. You're in a beautiful place among friends and I won't have you being sad."

I paused for a moment. I wasn't sure what to say.

"Thanks, Mary."

CHAPTER 6

THE FOUR OF US WERE SAT AROUND THE TABLE. There was enough food out to feed the whole of the island.

"Who was that John guy last night?" James asked. "He was convinced he knew me."

"Oh, John. Everyone knows John" Martin said. "He only lives down the road. He's a great guy. He used to drive the bus that goes past here. He's retired now though. Well, either that or he couldn't stay sober long enough to drive the buses anymore."

"You're one to talk, Martin."

Mary had a smile on her face. Unlike a lot of couples I'd seen, drinking wasn't a sore spot in their relationship. Mary just enjoyed teasing Martin.

Martin turned to James.

"That's something I always wondered about. In America, do they really drink from those red plastic cups? I don't remember ever seeing those when I was there. Granted, that was a long time ago now. Is it just that they can't show brand names on TV?"

James had spent a few weeks travelling across America with some of his university mates. I was incredibly jealous. I'd introduced James to Kerouac when we were younger. It had always been a dream of mine.

"It's funny, I actually asked someone that when I was there. I mean, in bars they obviously don't drink out of plastic cups. Apparently they do at parties though. They tend to just have kegs that everyone drinks from, so everyone needs cups."

"Kegs? Jesus. And everyone just shares?" Martin asked.

"That wouldn't work in Scotland, I can tell you that for free" Mary said. "The first person to get to the keg would be the only one who'd get anything from it."

I laughed. I started to worry I wasn't contributing to the conversation. Then I decided that Martin and Mary would probably rather catch up with their son than hear from me anyway.

Martin was starting to grill James a bit more on his U.S trip. He was very interested in what James had and hadn't done. They'd reached the topic of girls. Mary quickly changed the subject.

"So, Alex, are you happy to come to the ceilidh with us tomorrow? Isobel did ask you to come. You guys seemed to be hitting it off."

I knew what she was doing. I appreciated being invited into the conversation even if it was just as a distraction.

"I still don't know what a ceilidh is. But sure, if you're all going then I'll come," I said.

"You'll hate it," James assured me, "but we might as well go. It'll be funny."

"It's at the beach" Mary said. "If the weather stays like it is at the moment it'd be a crime not to go."

"There's not a lot of crime up here," James said. "They have to make up new crimes."

"It must be odd to live somewhere with beaches all around. Back home they seem like this rare thing you only get on holiday. It must be weird to have them just down the road" I said.

"Pfft. Wait 'til you see Harris. Harris makes Lewis look like Dresden after the war," James said.

"He's exaggerating," Martin said. "But it is more spectacular. That's where the biggest beaches are. They have the mountains too. So if we want to go to the really nice beaches we still have to do the drive down to Harris. But that doesn't exactly make Lewis a bombsite, not by any stretch of the imagination."

"So, what exactly is a ceilidh?" I asked, unsure if I was saying it right.

"It's like a big party," Mary said. "It's a tradition here. They play traditional music and everyone does all the dances. There's lots of different kinds of dances. Everyone has a drink and a good time."

"Not everyone does the dances," Martin said.

"Not everyone does the dances, that's true. Certain folk can never leave the bar for long enough to make it over to the dancefloor," Mary said, smiling.

"I'm happy to come. I don't think I'll be doing the dances though," I said.

"We'll see how it goes," James said. "I might need you as my partner."

"More than likely," Martin said. "What girl would want to dance with you?"

"With a loving father like you, why would I need the love of anyone else?" James replied.

"Right, if you've eaten enough now, I can hear Rupert running around in the garden" Mary said. "James, give Alex some wellies or something and you boys take him out for a walk. We need him tired by tonight so we can leave him inside when we go out."

CHAPTER 7

THIS WAS THE FIRST TIME I'D SEEN THE HOUSE IN DAYLIGHT. It was a beautiful spot. Across the road out the front was a sloping field with a few lazy sheep. The back of the house sat right on the edge of a loch. The back garden had a row of white stones dotted along the border. Just beyond was the water.

The water was completely, utterly still. Smooth, perfectly flat, reflecting the sky above. It looked like glass.

James had Rupert on a lead while we walked.

"So your parents basically have their own private loch?" I asked.

"Not exactly. If you look out there, that gap between the two rocks, that's actually wider than it looks, it heads all the way out to sea."

"Seriously? That's pretty cool. Does it get rough in the winter then? It must be pretty scary to have the sea out the back of your house."

"Dad says it never gets too bad. It's pretty sheltered so even when it's really windy it's not as if the water out the back gets that choppy. Sometimes it'll splash up into the garden but I don't think it ever reaches the house."

We were walking along a single track road away from the loch, heading down past where we'd left the car. To our right was a vast green hill. To our left was flat green land as far as the eye could see.

"So this is just public land? We can walk wherever?" I asked.

"I'm not really sure how it works to be honest. You see all those fences? I think that's just the farmers breaking up the land or something. There's always gates and stiles to let you get wherever you want to go. I think there's so much land here and so few people that you can pretty much walk wherever you want and not disturb anyone."

"That's really cool. It must be so peaceful living here."

"I guess it depends what you're after," James said.

"Yeah, I guess you're right. It's the everyone knowing each other that would get to me. I'd want more privacy. I guess that's where the fields come in handy though. Every time it gets a bit much you could just walk out to the middle of nowhere until you felt ready to see people again."

"Bit risky with the weather."

"I guess. It's just so beautiful though," I said.

"It's just fields, Alex. They have them everywhere. I can literally see three different kinds of animal shit from where I'm standing."

Rupert was off at the side of the track, squatting in the long grass.

"Make that four," James said.

"I know that. I don't mean the fields though. I mean

that there's nothing here. The sky looks so big. There's just so much blue. I've never really thought about it but all the buildings in towns block out most of the sky. You never get to see it all at once."

"Yeah, that's true. When it's sunny here it is really nice. If it stays clear tonight, it'll be good on the drive home. You'll be able to see all the stars. You won't believe how many stars there are when there's no artificial light lighting up the sky."

"A bit of me thinks I could really live here."

"You definitely couldn't. But still, it's good to hear you thinking up new things you could do with your life. You're not tied to anything now, remember, you can do whatever you like. Just don't move here. You'd go crazy."

It was the first time since we'd arrived that James had referenced why he'd brought me up. I didn't acknowledge it but I felt a surge of excitement. He was right. I could go anywhere. I had that money saved after all. I didn't have to wait for anything anymore. It's not like I liked my job. I wasn't bound to anything. I could always up and move to the Outer Hebrides if I wanted. Or somewhere else. Anywhere else. Wherever I wanted. Maybe somewhere with a few more people than the Isle of Lewis.

Rupert was tugging on his lead, desperately trying to get to something he'd seen in the fields.

"How old is Rupert?" I asked.

"About a year, I think. They got him just after I came up last year. He's a bit nuts by all accounts. He's just got too much energy. He's only young though. He'll calm down."

"It's a good place to have a dog. All this space to walk. It's not like you have to worry about cars going by or anything."

James bent down and let Rupert off the lead. He darted into the fields and stuck his nose down in the long grass, tail wagging madly. James told me he'd brought the dog whistle just in case Rupert ran off in the wrong direction. Apparently he did that sometimes.

We carried on walking down the track. Rupert had his nose to the ground. He was following one scent or another further and further in the opposite direction. We stopped and turned to try and work out what he was doing. James blew the whistle. Rupert stopped, looked up, looked around and then went straight back to whatever he was sniffing.

"Well, that wasn't exactly what I was hoping for," James said.

"I read this thing once, I've no idea if it works. Apparently if you run away from a dog it'll automatically run wherever you're running. I guess it's something to do with being part of the pack. Not wanting to be left behind or something."

"If he was that worried about being left behind he wouldn't leave us to go sniff sheep shit," James said.

"I guess you're right."

We started walking again. Rupert still hadn't budged.

"Oh fuck it. It's worth a go," James said. "It's not like anyone'll see us."

He blew the whistle again. Rupert looked up and James started sprinting. I chased after him. We were both wearing wellies which didn't help. After ten seconds or so James stopped and so did I. We turned around and saw Rupert hurtling towards us. Within a couple of seconds he'd caught up. He jumped straight against me, his front paws on my chest. I wrestled with his head a bit. He looked into my eyes, panting manically. James clipped the lead on and pulled him down.

"Maybe we should just leave the lead on. I can't be running like that again," James said.

"Fine by me. Imagine if we lost your parents' dog the first day here. I wouldn't even know how to tell them. Your mum still calls me the shoe-breaker. Imagine if I actually lost her dog. She'd still bring it up in a hundred years."

CHAPTER 8

OUT THE BACK IT WAS IDYLLIC. The water wasn't moving at all. The sun was just beginning to set and the sky was a pattern of different calm blues. I could've sat out in the garden all night.

Martin had offered to drive us. I figured it might've been an attempt to appease Mary after all her jibes about his drinking earlier.

I hadn't been sure what to wear. I had no intention of dancing so that didn't affect my choice. I just wasn't sure what was expected for something outside like this. Were you meant to wear wellies in case it was wet? Or were you meant to wear smart shoes and pretend you weren't ruining them? Somehow I settled on the latter.

The drive was about half an hour. We were heading somewhere called Seilebost. I think it's pronounced more like Sheila-bost. At least that's how I was saying it.

We weaved in and out of clusters of houses every five minutes or so. It would be overstating it to call them villages.

I looked at every house intently. They looked like they'd been there forever. I imagined the people living in them. Did they know how isolated they were? How far did they have

to go to get food? How did people live out here in the past?
Why did they all live so far away from each other? Surely they
weren't all farmers? I asked James about it.

"Fucked if I know," he said. I decided not to ask any more
questions.

I was starting to get used to the lochs sitting at the side of
the road. I couldn't get used to the sky though. It was huge.
This giant blanket over everything. I hadn't noticed how big
the sky was before. It was almost daunting. Comforting. But
intimidating.

We passed a large white house. It wasn't like any of the
others I'd seen. Out the front was some decking pointing out
to sea. The house had clearly been built with the view in mind.
It looked both spectacular and entirely out of place.

"I always think that's a bit of a shame," Mary said. "Why
bother moving here if you just want to live in a house that
doesn't fit in?"

I got what she meant. It definitely didn't blend in. Still,
if you'd give me the choice between one of the stout concrete
houses and that grand white monstrosity, I know which one I
would've chosen.

The radio in the car was inexplicable. It would jump from
Gaelic music to the Prodigy to S Club 7. It kept me on my
toes. Martin, sensing my confusion, explained that he couldn't
get many radio stations in the car when he was out driving.
Sometimes, he told me, he'd miss hearing the football because
of it. I pretended to understand what a tragedy this was.

"Still, it beats sitting on the M25," I said.

"That's true. That's one thing I don't miss," he said. "Even if it does mean I'm stuck with Island bloody FM."

We were driving alongside an empty green field when Mary told Martin to take the next right. We pulled in down a dirt track. We were next to a small colourful building. James told me it was one of the schools.

"Out here? There's only about five houses around," I said.

"There's a few of these schools all over the place," Mary said. "Some of them only have about ten pupils. A lot of them are closing down. The kids are all expected to go to the bigger schools in town. It's a shame but I guess it makes more sense. You can't have all the kids of different ages in the same class. It mustn't work at all. If you'd always lived here though I bet it would seem really sad. A woman at the hospital told me this is probably the last year this school will be open."

It was a strange place. There were a set of swings and the chalk numbers of hopscotch on the floor. One of the walls was painted blue with yellow swirling writing over it. There was a tarmac car park out the front probably big enough for five cars.

There were hand-made signs directing cars away from the school. Someone had put up tape to guide cars around to the field the other side of the building. The markings seemed fairly arbitrary. Beyond the far length of tape was just more empty field. There didn't seem to be any need to cordon off one bit of grass from the next.

It seemed like they had overestimated the numbers. The makeshift car park was pretty empty. We pulled up alongside a parked Range Rover and a man in a high-visibility jacket knocked on the window and told us we had to move in closer. Martin laughed but did as he was told.

We all got out of the car. I couldn't tell where we were meant to be going. I knew it wasn't in the school. A couple of girls sat at a table at the edge of the car park. Hanging off the front of the table was a large sheet of paper with the word 'Entrance' written in big blue letters next to an arrow pointing to the left. Mary handed them our tickets. I asked her how much the tickets had cost. She told me not to be silly.

We walked fifty metres or so across the grass. It was sandy and fairly sturdy so I felt like I'd made the right shoe choice.

I could see the panic of a few rabbits scattering across the fields. There were rabbit holes everywhere. In the distance I could see silhouettes of mountains. It was hard to tell how far away they were.

Soon the grass started to slant downwards and I realised where we were heading. We passed a large floodlight that made it easier to see the lay of the land. At the bottom of the slope was a flat patch around the size of a football pitch. At one end was a small gazebo with some microphones already set up. Around the edge were a couple of food stalls and a bunch of plastic tables and chairs. There were probably around fifty people in total – in very deliberate separate groups. It all looked a bit awkward to me. The meat smelled good though.

"I'm going to get a burger now," James said. "I bet they hardly brought any. If I don't eat now I know I'll be starving later."

"From all the dancing," Martin said.

"From all the dancing," James confirmed.

Mary and Martin went over to a group of people they knew. They all had plastic white cups. One of the women in the group was holding a bottle of wine.

James and I joined the queue at the burger stall. It was only a couple of people deep. To one side they had a pot of curry and to the other they had the barbecue with some burgers and kebabs on. I was intrigued by the curry but I couldn't work out how I'd possibly eat it. It seemed an odd choice.

"Traditional Scottish food," I said to James.

"Absolutely. Not a lot of people know that the curry was originally invented in the Outer Hebrides. They also invented the apple pie and the croissant."

We ordered our burgers. The guy told us it'd be a couple of minutes as he had to serve up a couple of curries first. I suppose it wasn't that unusual but it definitely felt it.

I looked up the slope we'd just walked down and saw a few more people arriving. There wasn't any music playing. It all felt a bit odd. Someone was in the gazebo fiddling with the microphones and a few other things. I could see a keyboard at the front, an acoustic guitar and maybe some fiddles at the back. I didn't know if that was all the instruments ready. I didn't know what the band would be like at all. Until then I hadn't even really thought about there being a live band.

Our burgers were handed to us on paper plates. I put the plate in the bin and took the burger in my hands. James did the same.

"Not too bad," he said.

"Yeah. I've definitely had worse. Especially from burger stands."

A little terrier ran up to James and began sniffing around his ankles. A few seconds later a bigger dog joined him. It was strange. Nobody seemed too concerned. I guess everyone had dogs so everyone was used to having them loose. These people either really trusted their dogs or didn't worry about them too much. If I'd had a dog I wouldn't have been able to relax if it was loose. I'd have been too worried about it bothering other people or sprinting into the dark and not coming back.

A middle-aged man was slumped in a plastic chair. He was surrounded by empty seats. He was drunk already. He must have turned up drunk, there was no other explanation. There was only the one beer at his feet. He was completely oblivious to what was going on around him. He shuffled in his chair and reached down for the beer can. He put it to his mouth and tipped the can completely upside down. He made sure he got every drop. When no more beer would come he simply dropped the can and let it roll down his legs to the ground. He smiled to himself, obviously content.

Mary was looking over in our direction. She was waving us, or at least James, over. He asked me if I wanted to come be introduced. I shrugged.

"Don't blame you," he said.

While James walked over to his parents I walked up the slope we'd come down earlier. I headed off to the side a bit and sat down on the grass. It wasn't too wet at least. I know if it had been lighter I would've been put off by all the rabbit shit. As it was, I didn't mind.

I looked over at the gazebo again. Nobody was fiddling with the microphones anymore. It was obviously ready for the band. I had no idea what time they were meant to start. I had no idea what time it actually was. I'd decided there was no point bringing my phone around with me. I didn't want to be contacted and besides, there wasn't signal on a lot of the island anyway.

I was curious about the darkness behind the gazebo. I was ninety per cent certain the beach was just down out the back but it was too dark to see. I didn't feel confident enough to wander over there on my own.

CHAPTER 9

I FELT A TAP ON MY SHOULDER. It was Isobel. She smiled at me. I felt embarrassed for sitting on the ground on my own.

"How's it going?" she said.

"Ceilidhs aren't exactly what I thought they were," I said.

"I don't think anyone knows exactly what they're meant to be like. They just make it up."

I asked who she'd come with.

"Oh, I drove down on my own. I thought it might be worth it. I've been to a couple of ceilidhs up here and they're usually pretty fun. I knew you were coming too so at least I knew there'd be someone else under forty here. I just say yes any time I'm invited out anyway. I can't stand being stuck in the accommodation on my own."

"Accommodation?" I asked.

She sat down next to me on the grass.

"Yeah, the nurses accommodation. Didn't you know that's where I was staying? I thought I'd mentioned it."

"You probably did. For some reason I kind of assumed you had your own place up here."

"You do know I'm not from here, right?" she asked.

I smiled at her.

"For christ's sake, Alex. Can't you tell the difference between my horrible Welsh accent and the lovely accent they have up here?"

"I guess. Now you mention it. To me it's just an accent though. There's no way I could pin point it."

"Of course. We're all the same to you English folk."

She laughed. I felt relieved.

"I've only been up here a month and a half. I'm just a locum. I don't work here full-time. I'm just plugging a gap. They needed someone to fill in for Speech and Language Therapy until they hire someone full-time. They've asked me to take the job but I'm not sure if I want it yet. Coming up here for a bit is one thing. Moving here is something else."

"I know what you mean. I've had a few moments the last couple of days where I've felt certain I want to live here. Then when I think about it I just can't picture it," I said.

"Oh look, movement."

Some figures were hovering over the instruments under the gazebo. They looked young. Surprisingly young. The boy at the keyboard said hello and launched straight into the first song. It sounded exactly how I expected it to sound. A middle-aged couple moved into the middle of the grass and began spinning each other around. A few teenage girls in wedge heels appeared from somewhere and began dancing too. I couldn't tell if it was ironic or not. I doubt they even knew.

"You up for stripping the willow tonight?" Isobel asked me.

"I might be. If I knew what that was," I said.

"It's one of the dances. They've all got names like that. There's set dances. I like it like that. You don't have to worry about being able to dance because everyone is doing the same thing."

"Surely you need some sort of rhythm though?"

"Maybe. I don't really know. I try not to think about it. I just bounce along to the music. It all sounds so happy I can't help but get into it."

"Maybe later. I'll see how I feel," I said.

The band had only been playing for a couple of minutes. I had a suspicion that the next hour of music wasn't going to sound too different.

"How about for now we just walk then? Get your legs moving and we'll take it from there. It's too cold to sit on the ground all night" Isobel said.

"That sounds do-able."

She stood up and offered me her hand. I stood up too. She did a little jig on the grass in front of me.

"The deal was walking."

"Just testing you."

We headed out over the back. Right where I'd been looking before. Behind the gazebo the ground slanted down sharply. The low light and the long grass made it difficult to get the next step right. The grass came to an end and there was a small jump down to the beach. Isobel placed her right foot forward and somehow glided gracefully down the sand onto the beach. I tried to do the same. I stumbled and had to hurriedly try and regain my balance. I ended up running five or ten metres past Isobel just trying to stay upright.

The wedge of sand behind us blocked out a lot of the music. The only light was from the moon. It felt almost eerie until Isobel caught up with me and wrapped her arm in mine.

A gentle but very cold breeze came in from the sea. I put my left hand in my pocket to try and warm it. I wanted to do the same with my right but Isobel's arm stopped me from doing so. I decided to sacrifice my other hand. It was worth it to feel like someone trusted me.

We started walking down the beach. We didn't discuss it, we just did. The music had almost completely faded. I started to hear the gentle lapping of the tide on the beach. I couldn't really see each wave so the sound seemed to exist entirely on its own. It was like hearing the pulse of the night. It was soothing.

Neither of us talked for the first couple of minutes. My eyes were adjusting to the blue light and I didn't want to do or say anything that would take us out of the moment. Eventually Isobel turned her head and spoke.

"I like seeing my footprints on the beach," she said.

I turned my head a little, careful not to untangle our arms. I could see both of our footprints heading back into the darkness. It was oddly satisfying. We kept walking.

"When it's like this it's easy to forget about the hassle of living here" she said. "If life here was just this then I'd never want to leave."

"It must be pretty nice to come up here for work though. Surely you could've ended up anywhere? It's not like it's some anonymous town."

"Yeah, you're right," she said. "I did my first year in Derby. It was pretty horrible. I didn't feel like I had any time to space out my own life. I was just another person in another town doing another job. Here's completely different."

She was speaking slowly. I wondered whether she had anyone else on the island she could talk to about her life here.

"Well, I'm glad you're here," I said.

I felt stupid. Neither of us spoke for another minute or two. I listened to the tide. I hoped I hadn't ruined the moment.

"The thing is, nobody told me why I was up here. You know, usually when you're a locum someone's just retired or someone's on maternity leave or something like that. With this, the woman who used to do my job had died. She collapsed suddenly at home. Nobody told me that until I got here," Isobel said.

"Jesus."

"Yeah. She lived on her own so nobody realised for a while."

I looked out to the sea. I wondered how far I could walk into it before the water was up to my mouth.

"I'd already started work before it came up. It was a teacher at one of the schools that told me. They told me one of the kids was finding the change difficult. He's got autism, you know, and he didn't like his routine changing. I didn't know what to say. I felt like I'd been tricked. I don't like feeling like I'm just filling a spot where somebody else should be. Does that make sense? I mean, obviously I'm not the victim of the whole situation. That poor woman is."

"Don't worry. I definitely get what you mean."

"It gets in my head a little too. Especially when the weather's bad and I'm driving on my own. What if something happened to me and nobody knew to look for me? I don't feel like I've worked here long enough to say to the department that sometimes I don't feel comfortable going out in the car. A couple of weeks ago it was really windy and I just had to hope someone else in the department would bring it up first. Luckily they did. I remember thinking afterwards how stupid it is that I was willing to risk crashing my car just to not have to bring up something I wasn't comfortable saying."

"Yeah. That is stupid. You've got to make sure you're safe. Think of it this way, at least you're not going to be here forever. Who cares if they think less of you? Why do they matter?"

"I know. But you don't have to work with them," she said.

I could see the faint trace of a smile.

"Yeah, you're right."

We walked another couple of silent minutes. I was worried we were running out of beach. When we'd first got down to the sand I couldn't make out where the beach ended. It looked like it might go on forever. Now I could see water in front of us. I was sad that we might have to turn round. I didn't want to face back towards the world just yet. Then I noticed the sand curving around to the right. The beach didn't end there. It kept going around the corner. The music was coming from within the dunes and the sand wrapped around two sides almost at a right angle.

At the turn the beach opened up even wider. We moved a bit closer to where the tide reached. Isobel's arm was still tight in mine. My hand was freezing. I could just about make out mountains across the water. In the dark it looked like there might be snow on top. I didn't know if that was likely or not. I decided not to ask. A group of birds flew overhead. They were pitch black V-shapes against a blue hypnotic background.

"Fancy a dip?" I asked.

"Oh yeah, right. Dancing is out of the question but swimming in the ice cold Scottish sea makes perfect sense."

"So that's a no then? That's a shame. I'm definitely up for it," I said.

"Oh really? Don't let me stop you. Go ahead."

"Nah. I'd hate to leave you on your own."

"Such a gentleman. I'm sure otherwise you'd be straight in the water."

My left foot sunk a little in the sand. I lost my balance slightly but pretended nothing had happened.

"I think solid ground is enough of a challenge for you tonight," Isobel said, laughing.

We were reaching the end of our new stretch of sand. Now we really were going to have to turn back.

"We could probably cut up through the grass there, if you're cold and want to get back," I said.

"Eager to get back are you? Can't wait to get dancing I bet. I'd rather walk back the same way if it's all the same to you."

"I'd definitely prefer that," I said, relieved.

We walked right up to the end of the sand. There was a large rock shining slightly in the dark. I could see the seaweed spread out over it. In silence, Isobel and I turned. We swivelled on the spot, parting arms for a moment. When our arms met again in the middle Isobel hooked on and we started walking again. My frozen right hand was free at last. I put it in my pocket, all the fingers totally numb.

We left a bigger distance between us and the sea on the way back. I think neither of us wanted to walk over our first set of footprints. It was re-assuring to see them alongside us as we walked.

We were both freezing but neither of us wanted to admit it. I started thinking about sleeping on the beach. It was obviously too cold. It would have been horrible. Yet something about the sound of the tide made me feel like closing my eyes and taking in nothing but the music of the sea.

I felt Isobel turn to say something. A seagull flew overhead and made a ridiculous noise that made me laugh. It stopped her from saying whatever she was going to say. I apologised and asked her what she'd been about to say. She told me it was nothing. We turned the corner back to the final stretch of beach. I could see the artificial floodlights lighting up the sky above. After a minute or two of gentle silence Isobel spoke again.

"I was going to say I'm glad you're here too," she said.

I felt gutted when I realised we'd finally run out of beach. It would've sounded stupid to suggest turning round and doing the whole walk again. It was even darker now and we were both clearly freezing. Still, if she'd suggested it I would have done it.

Isobel took her arm back and I rubbed my hands together quickly. My right hand was beginning to warm up but I couldn't feel my left hand at all. I took big steps back up the sand slope. At the top I turned around and pointed to Isobel the spots where I'd planted my feet. She took her own route which took half the time. She was annoyingly sure-footed.

The floodlights reached where we were now standing. I looked back to the sea. It seemed so far away. The beach was in total darkness. I couldn't imagine being down there again. I saw Isobel make her way back towards the music. I started jogging to catch up with her.

"Sorry," she said, "I've needed the toilet for about half an hour. I didn't want to say anything."

I worried she'd been uncomfortable the whole time we were on the beach.

"I think the toilets in the school are open, do you want me to walk you over there?" I asked.

"That's ok. You'd only slow me down anyway. The second you turn away I'm going to run. You go back and find James. He's probably wondering where you are."

I thought about walking back down to the flat grass but couldn't quite face the people yet. I pretended to head that way and saw Isobel start running back towards the school. Instead I reached the spot where Isobel had found me before and sat back down on the ground.

The music seemed to be exactly the same as it was when we'd left. There were more people dancing now though. A few of them seemed to know exactly what they were doing. Scattered around the edges were the less co-ordinated but no less enthusiastic. One couple were arm in arm spinning at a furious pace. I figured it had taken a lot of drink to get them to dance like that. I was certain the combination of spinning and alcohol meant at least one of them would be sick at any moment.

CHAPTER 10

THE DOGS FROM BEFORE RAN UP BEHIND ME. They sniffed around my back and then ran off again. I envied their energy.

I looked back towards the gazebo. The band sounded good. I think. They were definitely a tight group, I just couldn't get into it.

There was a young girl on the right of the group playing an acoustic guitar. I saw her moving awkwardly. She was trying to kick someone away. A drunk man seemed to be stumbling around her. She was still playing but she was clearly trying to get this man to move. Eventually he did move. He stumbled back away from the gazebo and after twenty metres or so he fell to the ground and stayed there.

The song finished. The girl with the guitar walked over to the boy at the front of the band and said something. The boy had a microphone attached to his keyboard. I hadn't heard any singing so I figured the microphone was just for addressing the crowd.

"Just to remind everyone," he said, "this is where the band plays, this is where our instruments are, this is where the speakers are. This is not a place for you to relieve yourself. No matter how desperate you are."

He laughed in a way that made me think it wasn't the first time that had happened. Then he announced the next song. He invited everyone to join in. I didn't know what was about to happen. Everyone congregated in the middle of the grass. They spread out into two single file lines facing each other. It happened slowly. The boy with the microphone offered a few more instructions I couldn't quite make out. A couple of women in the middle were dancing already even though the music hadn't started yet.

The band kicked into it. It didn't sound any different to anything else they'd played. The couple at the front of the lines began spinning each other around. It didn't look too controlled. They let go of each other and linked arms with the next person in each line and started spinning in the same way. It looked like the goal was to gain as much momentum as possible and then take off at the end.

Most people further down the lines were tapping their feet and clapping their hands while they waited for a body to be flung towards them. Some of them were paying no attention at all. One woman was so busy dancing to herself that she was facing the wrong way by the time it came for her to link arms. It meant the man ended up much further down his line than the woman did hers. I guessed it wasn't meant to be a race but it was starting to look like one.

I noticed some movement the other side of the gazebo. A young pair were walking out of the darkness. The girl was wearing a top with her stomach on show. She had her arms wrapped around herself and her shoulders scrunched up. The boy had his arm across her back. He looked like he was trying not to laugh. As they got closer to the lights the boy took his arm back. He walked away from the girl and headed over to a group of boys standing at the far end of the grass.

I kept my eyes on the girl. She kept her arms tightly wrapped around her stomach. She started speeding up. She was heading away from the music. She came towards me and then carried on up off towards the school.

"Don't tell me that doesn't look like fun?"

Isobel was back. She'd crept up on me.

"Come on," she said, "we'll just join at the end there. You won't have to do anything."

She took me by the hand and helped me up. I walked down the slope with her towards the music. I hadn't really agreed to anything yet. I hoped by the time we got there I'd have worked out something to say to get me out of it. I didn't.

The music carried on. The same tune going and going. The songs seemed to be built out of these endless bouncing spirals. We joined the end of each line, a few feet away from each other. Isobel was in her element. She was moving from one foot to the other and clapping along to the music. When she saw me put my hands in my pockets, she taunted me, putting one hand on her hip and swivelling around to the music, laughing.

I watched down the line. Nervously. The couple were still making their way up. I couldn't work out how they weren't dizzy yet. Maybe us people at the sides were just human walls to keep the spinning couple upright – grab them by the arm and hurl them back into the middle.

They were about three quarters of the way done. The girl had caught the guy up now so they were in roughly the same spot. I watched carefully to work out what I'd have to do. It seemed like I'd just have to lock arms, spin around and then let go. It didn't look too difficult. I was still anxious though. I had this horrible vision of doing it wrong. Messing it up somehow so that they'd have to start the whole thing over again.

I tried to count the number of people in each line to work out whether I'd be getting the girl or the guy. It looked like it'd be the girl. That seemed preferable for some reason. I looked over to Isobel. She wasn't trying to work anything out. She was happy dancing to herself.

Now they were coming for us. I realised I'd be getting the guy. I'd worked it out wrong somehow. He came right at me. I put my right arm out and he hooked on. We span around and then he let go. He went towards the girl, fresh from Isobel's spinning arm. They high-fived and hugged each other. The music kept playing. I waited for the song to build to a climax but it didn't come. I looked down the line. I saw the next pair, now at the front of the lines, beginning to make their way down the middle. It was never going to end. I was never going to escape. This must be how they spend the entire weekend. I looked over to Isobel. She was still dancing. I puffed out my cheeks and pointed over to the hill.

I felt a bit embarrassed for leaving. I didn't even look back to see if Isobel was coming. I sat down on the grass again and noticed a few other people spreading out a bit. They were starting to lose their patience too. Or their focus. It had been minutes since people had had a drink. They weren't going to stick to the rules of the dance if it meant missing out on drinking. I was relieved when Isobel came and sat down next to me.

"That wasn't so bad, was it?" she said.

"I guess not. That's it though. That's me done. That's my dancing career over."

"Well, you went out in a blaze of glory," she said.

"Thanks."

"Look, I really should get going now. I don't want to try getting out of the car park when all these drunks are pulling out too."

"I hadn't even thought about that. That sounds like a good idea," I said.

She wrapped her arm around me and squeezed. I tilted my head lamely in her direction. It wasn't much of a response. She jumped up, said goodbye and started walking to the rhythm of the never-ending music back towards the car park.

I looked out and spotted James eating another burger. It wasn't beyond the realm of possibility that he'd spent the entire evening devouring burger after burger. He always said he liked having something to eat if he was stuck in a boring conversation. It meant he could focus on the food and just offer enough signs of interest to make the other person feel like they weren't being ignored.

I stood up and started waving to him. He couldn't see

me. He was really focused on his burger. I started waving both arms over my head. Then I started jumping up and down. I figured if he couldn't see me, nobody else could, so I needn't feel embarrassed. He lifted his head up towards me. It took him a couple of seconds to register that it was actually me. He pushed the rest of his burger into his mouth and started imitating me, waving both arms over his head and jumping up and down. A few people nearby turned to look at him. He shook someone's hand and then started walking towards me.

He went close to the gazebo to avoid what had become the dancefloor. As he passed the band he clapped at them. The guy on the keyboard nodded in recognition. James made his way up the hill. At one point he slipped and had to put his hand down to catch himself. When he got to me he wiped his muddy hand on my shirt and laughed. He was pretty drunk.

"How's it going?" he asked.

"Not too bad. I think I've got the gist of it now though. I don't need to see any more," I said.

"Yeah. It's too cold to be outside now unless you're dancing like a maniac. And I'm just not capable of being a maniac, I'm afraid," he said, pulling a face.

"Of course."

We made our way back down, James clinging to me for balance. We found Mary and Martin and stood around for a few minutes while they said their goodbyes. They seemed to know everyone there. Each goodbye opened up five new avenues of conversation that took a long time to close. Eventually James just started tugging on Mary's arm. She apologised to the woman she was speaking to and said her final goodbye.

Martin and I were in front as we headed towards the car park. James was a few yards behind us talking to Mary. When their conversation finished they did a little jog to catch up. As James passed us he put his hands in the air triumphantly. Mary laughed and called her son an idiot.

"I am no idiot!" James said, "I am the most sensible man alive."

"No you're not. My lovely husband is. Look at him," Mary said, grinning and prodding Martin's face. "Not drinking just so we can have a nice time. What a gentleman. And such a handsome face. What a handsome, handsome face."

"I'd believe you meant that, if you weren't laughing while you said it," Martin said.

"I'm just in a good mood," Mary said.

We got in the car. Martin checked everyone had their seat belts on. There was a Porsche parked at an awkward angle. It made it difficult to pull out of the makeshift car park.

"Look at him, he thinks he's Rod Stewart," James said.

I laughed. The more James drank the more he started quoting things. I never could tell whether he knew he was quoting things or whether his brain, drowning in alcohol, simply reached a point where it wasn't capable of original thought anymore.

Within thirty seconds of driving we were surrounded by total darkness. I was pleased Martin was at the wheel. He was sober and he knew the roads well. I worried about all those drunk people back at the school. Some of them were definitely going to drive home. A couple of minutes on these roads in the dark was bad enough sober. Being drunk it would be just about impossible.

Martin braked quickly. Mary jolted in her seat and started to yell at Martin for scaring her. Then she saw the stag. It was standing in the middle of the road. Unmoving, it stared at the car. After a few seconds it wandered into the darkness. It was in no hurry.

"Christ!" Martin said.

"That didn't look anything like him," James said.

I didn't laugh. I was a bit shaken up. It really affected me. I wasn't sure why. I thought of all the miles of road winding all over the island. I thought of the infinite darkness and the lonely people trying to make their way home. It seemed awfully sad somehow.

James soon fell asleep. His snoring was the only sound in the car. Martin wasn't talking much and I didn't want to disturb him while he drove.

At last Mary spoke. She asked if I'd done any dancing.

"A bit," I said. Then it was silence again for the rest of the drive.

We pulled up at the house.

"Wake up kids. We're home," Martin said.

James opened his eyes. Without saying a word, he opened his car door and walked into the house. Back in the kitchen, Mary was fussing again. She offered me hot drinks and cold drinks and said she'd rustle up some sausages if I was even the

tiniest bit hungry. I promised her I was fine, I just wanted
to sleep. Martin had already gone to bed and Mary finally
relented and went to join him. I got into my room and took
off my clothes. They were cold to the touch, even on the
inside. I was pleased to be rid of them. I spread myself out
under the covers. I had too much on my mind to think about
anything clearly and fell asleep pretty quickly.

CHAPTER 11

MORNING. I could hear movement. Something about the layout of the house meant you could never tell exactly where sounds were coming from.

I wasn't sure how I felt. I wasn't really sure if I'd enjoyed the night before. It was something. It had made me feel something. That I was sure of. It felt like a start but I wasn't sure what it was the start of. I decided to take my time getting up.

I picked up one of my books and laid down. I straightened my back out on the hard floor. I liked to do that every now and then. I thought somehow it'd help my posture.

I tried to read but I couldn't really focus. I hadn't started any of the books yet. Having three with me made it impossible to start just the one. I'd start the first sentence of a book before deciding it wasn't the right book for that moment. Then I'd pick up another one. The same thing would happen. Then I'd move onto the next. I did this with each book two or three times. I felt like I needed something but I wasn't sure what it was.

I opened the door. No-one was on the landing. I tried to make it to the bathroom. I'd passed the stairs when I heard Mary give a ten minute breakfast call.

"I'm just jumping in the shower then I'll be straight down," I said.

"Put some clothes on after too," Mary replied.

I heard James' voice from somewhere in the house. "Clothes too! It's like a prison camp here."

I locked the bathroom door and took a few deep breaths. I felt like I hadn't slept but I knew I had.

I showered, got dressed and headed downstairs. Mary was rattling around in the kitchen. The room smelled great. She laughed off my suggestion of helping and told me to sit down. Again, Mary put out enough food to feed ten. It was like she had no sense of what was an appropriate amount of food for a normal person to eat in a sitting. She gave us each a plate with four beef sausages, three pieces of bacon, two fried eggs, mushrooms and an ocean of baked beans. That was just the first servings. In the middle of the table was an entire plate of extra sausages, an entire plate of extra bacon and a big bowl of baked beans. When I sat down she said she hoped it was enough. I laughed. She genuinely didn't seem to realise how generous she was. She poured us all orange juice and only sat down when we all loudly refused to start eating until she joined us.

"You boys got much planned for today?" Martin asked.

I didn't know the answer.

"I'm not sure yet. I've maybe got an idea if the weather stays ok," James said.

"So mysterious, my son. Don't keep us all in suspense!" Mary said.

"Well, are our neighbours still about? You know, Rupert's friends?" James asked.

"I think so, aren't they Martin?" Mary said.

Martin agreed that they probably were. I didn't want to ask who 'they' was. I was worried I'd missed something someone had said while I'd been busy shovelling sausages down.

After we'd tried our best to work our way through everything, we had to concede defeat. There was still a stack of untouched bacon. I noticed a slight hint of satisfaction in Mary's voice when she acknowledged there'd be leftovers. Rupert was delighted.

CHAPTER 12

JAMES TOLD ME TO WAIT DOWNSTAIRS while he ran upstairs to collect some things. I offered to help Mary clean the table in the meantime. Predictably, she told me to stay where I was. I got up and took a couple of plates over to the dishwasher. Mary loudly declared that if I kept it up she'd have to ask me to leave.

James came back. He was wearing a woolly hat and a pair of gloves. It seemed a bit over the top. It wasn't summer anymore but I could see that the sky was still a decent blue. He handed me some gloves and a hat and insisted I put them on. I didn't really know enough to resist. I started to wonder how far away these neighbours were going to be. For all I knew, island neighbours could be miles apart.

I eyed the camera bag over James' shoulder. It looked pretty expensive. He seemed to be angling himself out the back door so Mary wouldn't spot it. We'd reached the garden when Mary stuck her head out after us.

"Be careful with that James. If anything happens to it Dad'll kill you."

"I know, Mum."

I looked out at the water. It was peaceful. Just looking at

it made me feel calm. I took a deep breath and noticed James walking up the road without me.

We started out in a direction I hadn't been before. I realised we were heading down towards the water. About fifty yards from the house was an isolated shack. The windows were still intact but the paint on the walls had peeled so much it looked more brown than the original white. I thought maybe there was something inside we needed. That wasn't where we were headed though. James walked around to the other side of the building and I followed. There was a wooden path leading down, a bit slippery from the water. The path led out to a little deck at water level. There were a few boats scattered around. A white, expensive looking speedboat. A couple of small plastic boats that looked more like sleds. A very old fishing boat.

We were looking near enough directly back on James' parents' house across the water. It looked so much smaller from the outside.

James took off his gloves and put them on the decking. He reached into the water, grabbed a thin blue rope and started pulling. A small, red plastic boat began inching towards us. James pulled until it was within reach. He bent down and untied a couple of things.

"I'll get in first. Then you pass me the camera. I'll put it down. Then you step in. It's not too tricky. I'll hold you when you step over just in case."

James put his right foot down onto the red plastic floor of the boat. He swivelled his left leg around his right and planted it down firmly. He turned to face me.

"Now the camera."

I handed it over to him. I made sure James had a hold of it with both hands before I let go. The boat was moving slightly. I noticed it was about a metre further away from the decking than when James had stepped in. The camera had made it over ok. I wasn't so confident I'd manage the same myself.

I watched the boat carefully. I led with my right foot. The boat seemed to float further and further away. The water was hardly moving but the boat seemed determined to make it as difficult as possible for me. I felt my right foot reach the bottom. The boat moved under my weight. James reached out, grabbed my right arm and pulled me over. Suddenly I was pressed right up against James. He laughed.

"Welcome aboard. Take a seat just behind you," he said.

I carefully turned around. It was trickier than I expected. I felt more at ease once I was sitting. The boat was all red plastic. It had two benches across the middle. This meant that if you wanted to move from one end to the other you'd have to step over the two benches on your way. I decided I'd avoid moving and stay seated as long as possible.

At the back was a small motor. James sat next to it and got us started. I couldn't work out which way I was meant to be facing. If I faced backwards I could see James but not where we were going. If I faced forwards I could see where we were going but had my back to James. There was no way to sit sideways without having your feet up on the bench. I definitely wasn't doing that. I wanted my feet planted as firmly to the bottom as possible. I decided to face James and pretend to be interested in whatever he was doing.

He rested his hand next to the motor and seemed to be moving something small to steer us. We slowly moved out of the loch. I couldn't see the house anymore. We moved between the two rock banks and found ourselves in much wider water. We were in a long, straight stretch. Up ahead was a stony bank. Right seemed to curve back around out of sight. Left carried on between two hilly bits.

I could see a series of what looked like cages in the water. I asked James what they were.

"For catching lobsters. Or seaweed. Or mackerel or something."

"It's that sort of insight normal tourists miss out on. I'm lucky to have a guide like you."

"You are. You just don't know it yet," James said.

"I was thinking, maybe we should try and buy some food today and cook dinner tonight or something. I feel bad about how much your mum's been doing."

"And where do you think we'll be buying this food?" James asked, smiling.

"Can't we drive back into town? It wasn't too far."

"You miss my point. What day is it today?"

"Sunday" I said.

"Exactly."

"You're kidding."

"Nope. Not even Tesco is open. Nothing is open. It's a big deal here. They don't like people doing stuff on Sundays. My dad walks Rupert the same way every morning. He says the neighbours always wave to him or come out and say hello. Not on Sunday though. They just ignore him. They think he shouldn't be out. You're not meant to do anything on a Sunday" James said.

"That's mad. It's so rude too. I guess it could be kind of nice to know you've got that day to do nothing, but still, that's just mad."

"I know. Apparently it wasn't that long ago they used to chain up the parks here so kids couldn't even play on the swings on a Sunday."

"Jesus," I said.

"Yeah. It's his fault."

Talking to James calmed me a bit. I was getting more used to the motion of the boat. We were still moving forward pretty slowly. James took us alongside the cages in the water and around the right curve. He was good at steering. It was a smooth turn. He didn't even seem to be concentrating that much.

I was glad to be wearing my gloves. There wasn't that much wind but sitting down at near-water level made the air absolutely freezing. I could already feel my nose and ears all red.

"Do you see them yet?" James asked as we came out of the curve.

"Who?"

I was looking as far round as I could without moving from my seat. I couldn't see anyone.

"Turn around you idiot. Stand up and turn round

properly," James ordered.

I stood up. I felt the boat wobble under my weight. I got my balance and stayed standing as the boat inched forwards. We were in a narrow channel of water now. It was pretty calm. There was a white rocky cliff to one side and a grassy field to the other. In front of us was a kind of muddy patch where the water met the land. I could see some movement on the mud. I couldn't tell what it was though.

James slowed the boat right down. He told me he wanted the motor to be as quiet as possible. I stared straight ahead. I could see these touches of movement but I still couldn't work out what it was. I kept getting distracted by the waves to the side. Each splash against the white rock caught my eye. I was facing the wall of white when I saw something dark pop up out of the water and drop back down. It looked like a ball or something.

"Something just came up over there," I said.

"That's good. It means we've not scared them," James said.

James gently took us forward. We gradually got closer to the mud. The combination of the quiet air and the gentle rocking of the boat was kind of hypnotic.

At last my eyes tuned in. I could see three long smooth bodies on the mud. I could see a pair of black eyes looking back towards me. There was a group of seals lying out in the sun.

"This is mad. I've never seen seals before," I said.

"Look, there!" James said, pointing to our left.

There were some wide, smooth black rocks a few feet

below the grass. Spread across were what must have been over twenty seals I somehow hadn't noticed yet. The motor was still quietly purring away. As James moved us closer four or five seals rolled off down into the water out of sight. The rest didn't seem bothered.

James turned the motor off. We floated silently, the boat delicately bobbing up and down. James didn't speak so I didn't either. I watched the gang on the rocks. They didn't seem too put out. I wondered how often they saw people. They actually weren't too far from a little road. It just would've been impossible to know they were there from above like that.

Something moved in the corner of my eye. Two heads were up above the water. It reminded me of meerkats standing up and peering around. Just as I saw their faces they both popped back down beneath the surface. About ten metres further back a single head came out of the water. I couldn't tell if it was one of the previous pair. I hadn't seen enough of them to tell them apart. The idea of the water all around us being full of seals was kind of peculiar.

I stared at the head. It was strangely human. I whispered to James.

"This is so cool. Look at that one there. They're weird aren't they? They kind of have people faces."

"I think it's the eyes," he whispered back.

James started fiddling around with something. I turned around and saw him holding the most expensive looking camera I'd ever seen. The lens looked like a weapon.

"Let's swap seats," he said. "You come back here. Sit by the motor. I want to try and get some photos of them. They're hardly moving. I should be able to get some good ones."

He stood up and took a step towards me. I put one foot over the bench. I balanced my weight evenly on each foot either side of the bench and James sidled past me. He had the camera in his water-side hand. He wasn't even looking at it as he passed me. I waited to make sure he'd sat down safely before I began moving again. I was really worried about that camera.

I sat down next to the motor and inspected it. It was so small. It was strange how simple it all looked. The boat didn't feel like much more than a plastic trough floating on the water. The motor looked like it might fall apart in a strong wind. I knew that couldn't be true though given the winters it must've faced.

James was sat at the front of the boat, the camera pointed at the gang of seals. A few of them were looking over. They didn't do anything to indicate they'd actually seen us. They were just staring lazily in our general direction. Every now and then one would roll over into the water. Each time I'd hear James swear under his breath. I guessed he was trying, unsuccessfully, to catch an action shot.

A head popped up about five metres directly to the right of us. It looked right at me. I waved and it popped straight back down. It made me laugh. It was like they didn't like being caught. A few seconds later it popped back up again. I was starting to think of them as nosy creatures. Their faces suited that. They weren't too expressive but somehow that made it funnier.

I laughed again when it dived back under the water. James turned to see what I was laughing at and I pointed to the spot where the seal had been. The head appeared again a few metres to the right of where I was pointing. It was definitely looking at me. James tried to take a quick picture.

"I want to get one of them looking right into the camera," he said.

"Yeah, that'd be really good. I think their faces are really funny."

We sat in silence a minute or two longer. James had the camera ready in case he needed to pounce. There was something surreal about the boat rocking from side to side. It was only gentle, but in complete silence it took on extra significance somehow.

A bird flew above us honking loudly. I looked up at the silhouette of it against the sky. The wings looked huge. I wondered what kind of bird it was. I knew they had eagles in some places in the North of Scotland. As it got further away I could see it was only a large seagull. I felt like a bit of an idiot. I was pleased I hadn't acknowledged it out loud. It did look pretty impressive though.

James was still focused on the water. A breeze chilled my neck. I started to wonder how long we'd been out in the boat. On the ferry over to the island I hadn't even really felt like we were at sea. The arcade games and the pets and the pint glasses made it feel more like a shopping centre than a chunk of metal floating on the ocean.

I thought about the people working on the ferry. Out at sea for ages. I couldn't imagine doing it. I'd never feel settled. No matter what happens to you on land there's always more land to escape to. You can find a new patch of something solid and sturdy to walk or lie down on. At sea there's no escape. The boat can move across the water but you can't leave the boat. You're one of a million things out on the water the sea could push under whenever it pleases.

I watched a bottle-cap float past and realised my mind was wandering. The sound of a seal slapping against the rock as it clambered out of the water brought me back to the present.

I still didn't want to speak until James did. It was rare to see him concentrating on something like that so I didn't want to be the reason he snapped out of it. When he finally did speak, he was so casual it was like he didn't realise how long he'd been silently staring at the water.

"Mum was saying this morning, she bumped into that Isobel in the school toilets last night. She was saying how nice you'd been to her. She said you seemed cool."

"Cool?"

"I don't know. Something like that. I doubt my mum said cool. That was the gist of it though. Something positive."

"I'm sure she was just being polite."

"Oh here we go. Ian Curtis is back again. Why are you sure she was just being polite?"

"I hardly said anything to her. It's not as if she's going to tell your mum I'm a dick."

"Jesus. I'm not saying she said she wanted to marry you.

I'm saying she said you were alright. That's a good thing. It's not worth arguing about."

"I guess."

"Remember on the drive up? I said you should try talking to new people just to get out of your shell a bit. That you didn't need to worry so much about how you're coming across. You were all sulky and told me there's no point as you didn't have anything to offer people anyway. You said, and I think I'm quoting you right here, you said that no girl worth anything would give you the time of day."

"That sounds about right, yeah."

"How would you know? The last few years you've been wearing the same old rubbish watch. Girls can see you don't need the time of day. Of course they aren't going to give it to you."

"Very clever," I said. "When did you come up with that?"

"Look. I'm just saying Isobel thought you seemed nice. That's something. Maybe you don't come across as bad as you think you do."

"You're my friend and even you think I'm annoying."

"I think you're annoying because you're my friend. That's a totally different thing. Besides, that's not the point. God, you're being annoying right now. The point is, Isobel was saying she'd been talking to you and Mum asked her if she'd be happy to show you around town. Mum thinks it'd be weird if you never got to see Stornoway in the daylight. We've got loads more family coming round tomorrow and Mum said there's no point you having to meet a million people again. So she asked Isobel if she'd take you into Stornoway tomorrow. She said yeah."

"That's kind of her. Your mum I mean. And Isobel I guess."

"I definitely think you should go," James said. "If it's not shitty weather you can just walk around a bit. Besides, I don't want to have to introduce you to a million people. I won't be able to remember all their names and that always makes it awkward. I can't really have as many relatives here as Mum claims I do. It's insane."

"It is a bit mental. It's like people have three generations of the same family within a mile of each other. Then the cousins and in-laws just down the road."

"Yeah. It makes you understand why they're drunk all the time."

James raised the camera to his face and took a series of quick photos, moving around slightly after each click.

"You know what, if you want to steer us while we're moving, that way I can keep taking pictures."

"Is it easy?" I asked.

"Sure. You'll get the feel of it in no time."

I was already next to the motor. I couldn't really say no. There was a lever to one side of the box. I faced forward and rested my hand on it. I pushed down gently. The motor started to hum. We began moving very, very slowly. James told me to stay at that pace so we wouldn't scare the seals.

One by one the seals dived into the water. Even though we were moving incredibly slowly I was still worried about the rocks in front of us. I told James I was going to try and turn us. He said that was fine. I tried to turn towards the wide stretch of water. The boat went the opposite way I'd meant for us to go. Then I realised how the steering worked. I had to move the lever right to go left and left to go right. Once I'd worked that out it wasn't so bad.

I turned us while James kept taking pictures, adjusting himself as we swivelled around. I over-shot the turn a bit. Once you were turning it was tricky to stop exactly where you wanted to. Eventually I got us straightened up again.

James put the camera down and placed it back in the case. He told me I could speed up a bit now. It was quite satisfying hearing the motor go as we picked up pace. Curious heads still popped out of the water every now and then to see what we were up to. I tried to ignore them. I knew if I got distracted I'd do something wrong.

We were going along pretty smoothly back towards the opening near the house.

"You're a natural," James said.

He was joking, it was very easy, but it did feel good to get the hang of it so quickly. I could feel the boat moving up and down with the rhythm of the water. I wondered how fast it looked like we were going from the land.

We reached the opening and I got ready to turn. I realised I hadn't slowed down enough. I needed to turn quickly. Having to think quickly made me forget the steering pattern. In a panic I moved the lever the same way I wanted the boat to turn and we flung round the other way. I ended up having to take us around 270 degrees to get us on the right trajectory. I slowed the boat right down and asked James to do the last few metres up to the decking.

When I took my hand away it was so cold I could hardly move it out of the claw shape needed to steer.

My first step back on solid ground felt surprisingly heavy. I yawned while we walked back to the house. James was talking and I wasn't responding too well. Something about the sea air had made me sleepy.

CHAPTER 13

IT WAS GOOD TO BE INSIDE. I took a long shower to warm myself up. I hadn't felt like I'd needed to but James insisted. I was glad he did. It felt great. I always seemed to be showering in their house.

Of course, Mary was busy in the kitchen. It smelled fantastic. Mary was always preparing food before you even knew you needed it. Her cooking always smelled so good that even if I wasn't hungry I always would've wanted to eat anyway.

Mary ordered me to sit and brought me a glass of lemonade. It felt cold going down my chest which I took as a sign that I'd warmed up properly. James sat down and opened a bottle of beer. Martin came in and James told him to sit down. He passed his open, untouched bottle towards Martin and got up and got himself a new one. It was oddly touching. I wondered if I had instincts like that.

The table was slowly filling. Potatoes. Parsnips. Carrots. Broccoli. Yorkshire puddings. Stuffing. To finish Mary put down a massive chunk of roast beef. I couldn't wait to taste it. I felt hungrier than I'd ever been. I don't know if it was sitting with the smells or the cold sea air doing something funny to my bones but for a moment I couldn't think about anything else except that beef.

Martin served up the meat then Mary told us to help ourselves to the rest. She'd put a big serving spoon in each dish. I waited to see how much James took before I decided what was an appropriate amount of each thing.

"Did you have a good time on the water?" Mary asked me.

"Yeah. It was great. I've never been out on a boat like that before," I said.

"It's more of a bucket really," Martin said.

"Well, it does the job. And I've definitely never seen seals like that before" I said. "I expected them to be more scared of us. They just seemed curious."

"Did you really take Rupert out there once?" James asked Martin.

Martin laughed. Mary tutted.

"I wasn't here when your father did that. I got back and he showed me the photos he'd taken."

"He loved it. He had his paws up over the side watching the seals. He wasn't barking at them or anything. He just wanted to watch them. At one point I thought he might jump into the water after them. He didn't though. He was good as gold. He loved it," Martin told us, smiling.

It was the first time I'd heard Martin talk about Rupert. He seemed to love the dog. I figured he must do to take him out on the boat. It wasn't exactly a normal thing to do. It was sweet really. I tried to picture Rupert on the boat. It sounded like a recipe for chaos. He was enough trouble on land. From what I'd seen of Rupert he never stopped moving. If he'd been out with us I had no doubt he'd have knocked everything not tied down into the water. Including the camera. Including myself.

"It's a really good thing to be able to do that at the weekend," I said. "People would travel miles for that and you have it at the back of your house. I guess for you now it's no different than seeing a fox in your garden or something. I loved it though. I'd never get to do that back home."

"Well, it's not like there's much else to do on a Sunday," Martin said.

"Some of our neighbours don't like us using the boat on Sunday," Mary said.

"Really?" I asked.

"Oh yeah. Can't do anything on a Sunday. It was one of the first things they told us when we were moving in" Mary said. "Right after they'd introduced themselves. Don't even hang your washing up on Sundays. People don't like it. Well, I work the rest of the week and sometimes Sunday is the only day I can get things done. They can judge me all they want. It's not killing anyone."

"It's not that big a deal really," Martin said. "It's just funny when I'm walking Rupert. Six days of the week people wave out their windows then on Sunday they ignore me."

"I wonder if they ever wake up on Sunday morning and for a minute forget what day it is" James said.

"What about when Christmas is on Sunday?" I asked. "Is that good for them or bad? Are they allowed to visit family or do they have to sit at home because it's Sunday?"

It was strange to be talking about people not more than two hundred yards away as if they were from another planet.

"I don't know really," Mary said. "When I started at the hospital a woman told me that some people don't celebrate Christmas if it's on Sunday. I've never heard of anyone really doing that though. She might've been joking."

"I wouldn't put it past them. There are some odd folk around. Tell the boys about that woman and her horse," Martin said to Mary.

"What? Mum, if this is what I think it's going to be I don't think I want to hear this story come out of your mouth," James said.

I laughed.

"I don't even want to know what you boys are thinking," Mary said.

"Sorry Mum. Nothing. Come on, tell us about this woman and her horse."

"This lady, Irene, she's a receptionist on one of the wards at the hospital. I see her quite a bit so we have a chat every now and then. A couple of months ago I asked how she was doing and she said she was exhausted. She said her neighbour was driving her crazy. She lives in one of those two-storey grey buildings. She's on the second floor. There's a flat with someone else in on the ground floor and it's just the two of them in the building. She told me that the woman below her was a bit of a drunk. She said sometimes she'd hear the woman yelling in her flat even though she knew no-one else was there.

When she moved in Irene tried to introduce herself but the woman wasn't having it. So they pretty much ignored each other from then on. Irene said she was fine with it like that. Then, a couple of months ago…now this woman is really into horses. She had one in some stables somewhere and would go over and see it. How she ever managed to get on a horse when she was drunk all the time I've no idea. Anyway, apparently the people who ran the stables got tired of her. She'd turn up at the wrong time and demand everyone listen to her while she yelled about whatever. She'd obviously be drunk and park blocking the entrance. They didn't want her coming anymore. So they told her, you can't come back here. You're drunk all the time and we don't want to deal with it. Now the woman has two options. She can either leave the horse at the stables or she can find somewhere else to keep it. So, to this woman, it's a no-brainer. She's got a couple of rooms in her flat after all."

"You're kidding."

"I wish I was. So she brings it home. She gives up the living room to the horse completely. Lays down straw all over the place. She lived in the bedroom and the kitchen while the horse had the living room. Irene said it took her a few days to realise what was happening. She said she'd hear weird noises from downstairs but obviously she never expected that. Then one night she was coming home from work and she saw this horse through the window. She couldn't believe it. She said she nearly had a heart attack. She went and knocked on the door but the woman wouldn't answer, so she called the RSPCA about it. They said they wouldn't come out unless there was evidence the horse was being treated badly."

"It was being kept in a house by a drunk woman. Isn't that enough?" James asked.

"You'd think, wouldn't you? Anyway, a few days of knowing the horse is down there and she's getting pretty stressed out about it. It's probably quite hard to fall asleep when you know there's a horse a few feet below you. So, one morning she wakes up and her taps aren't working. She goes to the toilet and it doesn't flush. She calls up a plumber who says he'll be round in the afternoon. She calls up work and says she won't be coming in. So she's sitting in her flat waiting for the plumber. She can't wash and she can't go to the toilet. It's not nice. Eventually the plumber shows up and he checks the pipes and everything. Long story short, it turns out the woman downstairs had been shovelling the horse dung down the toilet. And when that got blocked she'd been forcing it down the sink instead. She completely blocked everything up with it."

"Jesus!" James said.

Martin was laughing.

"What happened to the horse?" I asked.

"I don't actually know," Mary said. "It was in the paper that the woman got arrested for drink driving. Irene said the flat's just empty now."

"Don't let that fool you though boys, most people here are pretty normal," Martin said.

"Sure sounds like it," James said.

"He's right. Most people have been really nice to us from

the minute we got here," Mary said.

"I'd fit right in here," James said. "I couldn't be a more polite young man."

"That's debatable!" Mary said. She then turned to me. "You know, I bumped into Isobel in the school last night. She was telling me how nice you were to her."

I tried to look calm.

"I told her how long I'd known you for. We were talking about how lucky it is the two of you met while you're up here. It really is. It's nice you've met someone younger to talk to. Don't get me wrong, I'm really happy you're here but I'd hate for you to have to spend the whole week being introduced to people twice your age."

"Yeah, I don't recommend it," James said.

"They're your family, James. That's why it's not a chore for you. It's a pleasure," Mary said.

"Of course it is, Mum. You're right. My mistake."

"Anyway, I told her that tomorrow we had lots of family stuff on and I was worried you'd be bored," Mary said.

I told Mary she didn't need to worry about me. She'd already done so much for me as it was.

"I'm not worried about you. I was worried you might get bored. There's a difference. Anyway, Isobel was keen for the two of you to do something together. I think she's going to take you around Stornoway. It's not especially big but it'd be a shame if you left without having seen it in the light."

"That sounds great, thanks Mary," I said.

"Don't thank me, thank Isobel. I think sometimes she

wishes there were more people her age around. Now, the buses aren't great out here so take our car. You two don't want to have to fill up again while you're on the island. The petrol costs a fortune here. Better to wait until you're on the mainland. Do you remember the way back to Stornoway? It's just straight back to where you came off the ferry."

"Yeah, I think so."

I wasn't certain I did know the way. I just felt the need to be as co-operative as possible. For some reason saying I knew the way seemed like the most helpful thing to do.

"It's not difficult," Martin said. "You just follow our road to the end then go right. You'll see Stornoway on the sign. Then it's just one long road all the way to town."

"Right," I said.

"Isobel said she'll meet you at the Co-op. Turn right at the first roundabout when you get into Stornoway, then the Co-op's on the left. It's pretty big. You can't miss it," Mary said.

"I'll just give James a ring if I get lost." I made a mental note to take my phone with me for once.

"You'll be lucky. I'll be having too much fun with all my elderly relatives to pay any attention to you," James said.

That night James and I watched a film. Some guy was smuggling diamonds from one place to another place. I couldn't really get into it. I felt nervous but I wasn't sure why. Luckily it didn't really matter to James whether I liked the film or not. It's always uncomfortable when someone shows you something they love and watches you intently to check if you're enjoying it too. This wasn't like that. James fell asleep towards the end so I knew he wasn't too into it either.

CHAPTER 14

I GOT IN MARTIN'S CAR AND PULLED AWAY FROM THE HOUSE. It was an unremarkable morning. The sky was a dull kind of blue. There was a canvas of clouds tightly wrapped around the sun.

I put the radio on. I could tell it was still tuned to Island FM before they even announced it. It was pretty unique. The adverts were sloppy. Unprofessional but endearing. They were for specific shops in Stornoway. Carpet sales. Pet grooming. Things like that. There was a jaunty kind of Gaelic piece that sounded like what they'd been playing at the beach. Then it was a Chemical Brothers song I couldn't remember the name of. It took me back to a night I'd spent in a club in Manchester. Kim had gone off somewhere and left me all alone. I was stood at the bar surrounded by strangers wishing I was anywhere else.

I hadn't seen any major turns or come across any roundabouts. I assumed I had to still be on the right road.

The Spice Girls came on. It made me laugh. I wondered if there was anyone on the entire island who'd enjoyed all the last three songs. I didn't change the station though. It put me in a good mood. It made me think of school discos. All the boys standing on one side watching the girls do their dance routines. Then later the DJ putting on that one slow song and everyone getting in position. Partnering up and standing in one long line. The girls have their hands on our shoulders and we have our hands on their hips. We rock awkwardly from side to side desperate for the song to end. We put on brave faces pretending we're comfortable with it all.

I reached a roundabout. There was a Chinese takeaway to one side. There weren't any signposts. I went right and saw a long stretch of road. Not busy by mainland standards but more cars than I'd seen anywhere else on the island. I didn't quite come to a stop but I did have to slow down a little. I wondered if it counted as traffic.

There was a big car park on my left. It looked like an industrial estate or something. It was hard to tell because there were trees blocking the view from the road. They kind of looked like palm trees but I knew that couldn't be right.

I reached another roundabout. I didn't remember Martin mentioning a second roundabout. I looked back over my left shoulder and realised I'd just passed the Co-op. That big car park was where I was meant to meet Isobel. I went all the way round the roundabout and drove back up until I saw the turning for the Co-op. I pulled over and chose a space near the front of the shop. I wasn't sure what I was meant to do next.

CHAPTER 15

I WENT TO THE CASH MACHINE JUST TO BE DOING SOMETHING. I took out ten and it gave me two fivers. Always a pleasant surprise. As I took my card back I felt a tap on my shoulder.

"You drove straight past me," Isobel said.

"Sorry. I didn't see you."

"Of course you didn't. I didn't think you were just ignoring me."

She gave me a hug and began walking. I followed. I decided not to ask where we were going.

At the front of the car park was a large wooden bull. It had been carved with incredible detail. It was so big up close it was actually kind of intimidating. There were a couple of seconds of silence while I wondered why it was there. There was no sign next to it. No explanation of who had made it. It surely wasn't anything to do with the Co-op.

Isobel asked me if I'd seen any real life highland cows yet. That made much more sense. It was a highland cow. I didn't let on that I'd thought it was a bull. I told her I hadn't seen any highland cows yet. Then I told her about the seals.

"I'm so jealous," she said.

She managed to combine envy with enthusiasm in a way I hadn't really seen before. She genuinely seemed excited for me. So much so that she wanted to do the same thing herself. Too often when people say "I'm so jealous" they seem to infuse it with a kind of resentment. With Isobel that wasn't the case. There was no bitterness. No sadness. Just joy.

"I've seen dolphins here," she said. "It was surreal. Have you been over to Tolstadh? I was walking along the long beach up there and I saw these fins popping up out of the water. At first I thought it might be my mind playing tricks on me. You know the way the waves sort of overlap each other? I thought it might just be that. Then I saw five or six of these fins at once. They do this sort of slow loop thing as they move through the water. It's really smooth. I have to admit, I think they were actually porpoises, but it sounds more exciting to say dolphins."

"It definitely does. I've never seen dolphins anywhere. Or porpoises," I said.

"When I was in America I got to swim with some," she said. "It was all arranged so it's not quite as wild as it sounds. It was still amazing though, don't get me wrong."

"Is it like they say it is? Is it one of those things everyone has to do?" I asked.

"I mean, your life isn't empty if you haven't done it. I wouldn't fly over to America just to do it. That would cost loads. If you have the chance though, there's definitely something about it. It's not like being surrounded by fish. Fish feel kind of automatic. You don't connect with them.

Dolphins though, you feel like you're interacting somehow."

We were following the pavement down the left side of the road. We crossed at the roundabout I'd gone all the way round a few minutes before. There were some banners tied to the fence at the side of the road. Margaret was fifty today. Donald and Fiona had been married thirty years. Tom and Hannah welcomed Freddie to the world. There was something charming about these very personal messages sitting right in the middle of their biggest town.

The other side of the road looked more interesting. There were these little flowerbeds in front of a thin layer of trees. Between two of the thicker trees stood a stone archway. There didn't seem to be anything behind it. I wondered if there had been a castle there at some point. I was kind of disappointed we weren't heading that way.

We carried on talking as we walked. We passed a few charity shops. A pet grooming place. The one from the radio. An old looking Harris Tweed shop.

"Are we in actual Stornoway yet?" I asked.

"Yeah we are. It's only a couple of minutes across really. I guess we're not technically in the town centre yet but this is all Stornoway. Over there's Stornoway Castle. Actually, I think it's called Lews Castle. Lews. Not Lewis," she said.

To the other side of the road was a narrow stretch of water. It didn't quite reach the banks at the side which left long patches of the dirty bed on show. It was the one blip on the scene. As we moved further down the castle came into view. There was a clean patch of green grass sitting in front of the small, surprisingly tidy-looking castle. The whole thing was framed perfectly by the trees.

"Have you gone in the castle?" I asked.

"You can't. It's a shame really. I like castles. I like wandering round them. But they've been doing it up as long as I've been here. It was only a few weeks ago they took the scaffolding down from outside. It looks much nicer now but you still can't go inside. I think they're going to make it into a museum or something. I hope so anyway. It'd be sad if they sold it off just to be some offices or something like that."

"Yeah it definitely would. It's cool that it's just there in the middle of town," I said.

"Yeah it is. Do you know what time you're heading back today? I don't think Mary said they'd be busy all night, we probably won't have time to see all the castle grounds. We definitely should at some point though. It's crazy how big it is."

"That sounds great."

Still walking, I watched the castle as it moved out of view again. Aside from the grass at the front I couldn't really see anything that would count as the castle grounds. Still, I trusted Isobel. If she said it was worth exploring then I knew it was worth exploring.

The town centre was very small. You could stand in the middle and read the names on the front of each shop in every direction. That's how few there were. There was a Boots and a Superdrug. And an Argos. I figured as there was no competition this was probably the one place in Britain Argos could still do a decent amount of business. The library looked quite nice from the outside but it was shut. The hours in the window told me it was shut every Monday. That didn't seem right.

We took a left into a pedestrianised square in front of a church. We headed into a modern-looking glass building on the right of the square. The one I'd seen from the ferry. There was a reception area and a shop selling the sort of things tourists buy. Over-priced jewellery. Birthday cards with fancy cartoons for four pounds each. That sort of stuff.

"Without this place I don't know what Stornoway would be like," Isobel said. "Through there's an art gallery. Upstairs is a bar. And a restaurant. And it's the cinema and the theatre and they have gigs here too."

"It doesn't seem big enough for all that," I said.

"Oh, yeah, that's because the cinema is the same room as the theatre. That's where they have gigs too. They just take the chairs out."

I peered through to the art gallery. There were various photo portraits on the wall. Sheep. Hills. Isolated buildings by lochs and so on. I figured if there was one place in the world where the locals didn't need to see pictures of that stuff it was here.

We headed upstairs. The walls of the bar were covered in movie posters. They weren't for classic movies. Or particularly new ones. It seemed to be a random assortment of whatever they could get their hands on.

Through the bar was the restaurant. We sat over by the

window. It looked down onto the harbour where the ferry had pulled in. The water wasn't too choppy. It was a pretty nice view.

"So, do you go to the cinema here much then?" I asked.

"I did when I first got here. The thing is, they only show films at the end of the week. I like to do other stuff at the weekends. It's difficult for me anyway, there's not much for kids to do here so they all go to the cinema. It means when I come I end up surrounded by kids I know from work. It makes it kind of awkward."

"I can imagine."

The waiter came over and gave us our menus.

Isobel laughed.

"Sorry Alex, I just realised I've not explained to you what we're doing at any point today. You've just had to follow me wherever I walked. I figured we would come here for lunch," Isobel said.

"I worked that out, thanks."

"Alright, yeah, I know. I mean, it's somewhere nice and warm to sit and talk for a bit. And the seafood soup here is great. I don't know the rest of the menu but if you want something filling for lunch that soup can't be beat."

"I'll trust you on this."

Of course, she was right. It was fantastic. I guess the seafood had only travelled about fifty metres from the water to our table. We didn't talk about anything too serious while we ate. I liked that.

The rain started before we finished eating. It banged against the window. By the time we asked for the bill it seemed to have quietened down a bit. We worked out I still had a couple of hours to spare. As we walked back through town Isobel suggested we head to hers. The rain had stopped momentarily but it didn't look like it would be long until it started again. She said her place was pretty near so we could take shelter there. I agreed. We made our way back to the Co-op car park. She'd walked down to meet me so I drove us both over to hers. It was only a minute or two down the road.

CHAPTER 16

I MUST HAVE VISITED UNIVERSITY HALLS more than anyone who hasn't actually been to university. Isobel's place felt exactly like university halls. It was strange to think of her staying somewhere so bland. I always felt like interesting people have to live in interesting places where interesting things happen or they'll end up like everyone else.

She was staying in NHS accommodation. She told me sometimes medical students doing their training at the hospital would stay there rather than find their own place to rent. We were standing in the living room. I told Isobel the place looked pretty tidy for somewhere a bunch of students were living.

"Oh no, there aren't any students here now," she said. "That's why it's so bare. There's only me here. There's only been one other person the whole time I've been here. This doctor guy. He was quite old and a bit funny. Sometimes I'd be cooking my dinner in the kitchen and he'd come in and talk to me. Sometimes I go to the gym after dinner and he always asked me what I'd be doing at the gym. One time I told him I was going swimming. Then later when I was swimming I saw him sitting in the cafe they have there that looks down at the pool. It might've just been a coincidence but it weirded me out at the time."

She laughed, which gave me permission to laugh too.

"I'd rather the place was empty than it just be me and him," she added.

She took me through to her room. There was an open suitcase on the floor with folded clothes in it. There were various wires and things tangled up on the desk. The walls were bare and the bedding was plain. There were some books on the floor under the desk.

"When you're back on the mainland, forget about this bit. Remember all the beautiful bits of the island instead," Isobel said.

"I'm glad to be here."

"Well, that's good to know, because you don't have a choice. Now, what could make your holiday any more special? I know. Watching bad T.V until James is free again?"

"For now all I want is to know where the toilet is," I said.

"Just there on the right," she said, pointing down the corridor.

When I got back to the living room Isobel had put a few things out on the table. An open bottle of red wine. Two cans of coke. A bottle of Irn Bru. Some chocolate fingers. A few packets of crisps.

"I wouldn't have had lunch if I'd known you were putting on a spread," I said.

"Don't take the piss. I didn't know if you wanted anything, so I just grabbed everything. It's not too early for wine is it?"

"It's never too early for wine," I said. "Except … I've got to drive back later."

"Of course you do. Sorry, I'm an idiot. I don't often have people over so I got excited at having someone to share wine with."

"You still go ahead. I'll have some Irn Bru in my wine glass so you don't feel like the only one drinking," I said.

"A fine choice, sir. Perfect for the man looking to develop attention deficit disorder," Isobel said, pouring me a glass of alarmingly orange liquid.

"Is it true that coke's the most popular drink everywhere in the world except Scotland because everyone drinks Irn Bru here?" I asked.

"I don't know. I'd believe that though. In my first week here I picked up a bottle and couldn't really stomach it. That's why there's some left for you to enjoy, you lucky guy. I just felt the need to buy it when I saw it. It's such a hypnotic colour. I remember I bought this haggis pizza too. I don't know why. It didn't taste of anything. I guess I thought I was being Scottish. Luckily since then I've gone past Tesco to experience Scottish culture."

"Kilts and whisky?"

"Some weekends, yeah. Now quiet, we're missing Deal or No Deal," Isobel said.

I opened a packet of crisps. The woman on screen opened her box to reveal 50p. Everyone looked devastated. I crunched on a crisp.

"How can you eat at a time like this?" Isobel said.

I asked Isobel a few more things about her life here. She seemed to have a decent routine. She went swimming most evenings if she didn't have anything else on. She knew enough people to get invited to things but didn't know anyone well enough that she felt bad about turning invitations down. She said she liked doing things on her own sometimes. She said walking the beaches on her own was one of her favourite things to do. She told me I had to go out to Tolstadh even if I ended up going alone.

We were deep into a Come Dine With Me marathon. Isobel was getting sleepy. She rested her head on my shoulder. I tried to crane my eyes around her forehead to see if her eyes were open. I wasn't sure if I wanted her to be asleep or not. I didn't want to have to wake her but I liked the idea of her trusting me enough to sleep on me.

Eventually, Isobel spoke, sounding sleepy.

"Are you desperate to find out who wins? If not can I change the channel? Every time I get comfortable one of these people says something ridiculous and it wakes me up again."

She lifted herself off my shoulder and moved the other way. Her head was on the arm rest and her feet were pressed up against me. She wasn't wearing socks. I made sure my hands weren't near her bare skin.

I looked at the clock on the mantelpiece. It was a small, grand looking thing.

"Is that your clock?" I asked.

"That one up there? Oh yeah, I never go anywhere without my hundred-year-old clock," she said.

"If it's right, I need to get going," I said. "I don't want to get back too late. Besides, you could probably do with going to bed."

"Yeah, I guess. I'm not in work tomorrow either so I was planning on either sorting out my room or catching up on some sleep. Maybe if I go to sleep now I'll get up early and get some stuff done. Or if I'm honest I'll probably end up sleeping all tonight and all through tomorrow too."

"Sounds good to me," I said.

Isobel lifted herself from the sofa and followed me to the front door.

"I won't come out to the car if that's ok," she said, yawning.

"I think I'll be alright making it ten metres on my own."

"That's right. You're a big boy after all."

"Well, thanks for dinner," I said.

She leaned in and hugged me.

"Don't forget about Tolstadh," Isobel said.

"I won't."

I sat down in the car and looked back at the front door. It was already closed.

I turned the key and the radio started. Pulp were just finishing. Next it was bagpipes.

CHAPTER 17

THE KITCHEN TABLE WAS COVERED. There was a big hiking backpack on the floor with two roll-mats crammed in the top.

Martin came in carrying a cool-box.

"I don't know why he thinks you'll need this. Just leave your drinks anywhere and they'll stay cold. We're not in Hawaii for Christ's sake."

At the hospital I always hated it when someone came into my office unannounced. They'd always expect me to deal with some situation I knew nothing about. It brought something out in me – something between resentment and embarrassment. I was no good at being thrust into situations I wasn't in control of. For some reason though, on the island, I didn't mind being out of the loop so much. I had this feeling that whatever was about to happen, it wasn't anything to worry about.

James came in wearing a woolly hat. He spoke to me first.

"You're back. Great." Then he turned to Martin. "Oh, thanks for that Dad."

"I don't know why you want this. Just put your drinks down anywhere. They're not going to get warm," Martin said.

"What about the food?" James asked.

"Why will the food magically get warm?" Martin replied.

"Good point. I guess you're right. We'll probably cook as soon as we get there anyway. That cool-box takes up so much space it's probably better to leave it here. I'll try and fit everything in the bag instead."

"So you won't be needing it then?"

"Sorry Dad."

Martin exhaled loudly and carried the cool-box out the back door again.

"Go put on another layer or two. Just in case. I think I've nearly got everything ready," James said.

"What sort of-" I started.

James cut me off. "-not now mate. Just go get ready."

I went upstairs and pulled a red fleece from my bag. I was now wearing a t-shirt, a jumper and a red fleece underneath my jacket. In the warmth of the house it felt ridiculous. I had no idea if it was enough for where we were going.

James slid a crate of beer into the top of the camping bag. It was pretty full.

"I think if one us carries this and the other one carries the wood then that should be everything," James said. He bent down and picked up the bag. It looked heavy. "Oh, can you grab that bit of paper off the table? And the torch too. Just in case it's dark. There's a bag of wood by the back door up against the wall. If you can take that to the car then that's everything."

We were taking Martin's car. James said he should drive as

he thought he knew the way. Besides, he said, he was planning on drinking through the night so I could do the drive back in the morning.

"Now can you tell me where we're going?" I asked.

"It's not a secret. I've just not been there before either so I'm not sure exactly how to describe it. My dad drew us a map on that bit of paper."

On the top of the paper was the word BOTHY. Beneath was a not very clear sketch.

"I'm not exactly sure what this is meant to be," I said.

"It's alright. It's only in case we get lost. I know where we're parking. It's just once we're out of the car I might get confused."

"Are we camping?"

"Not exactly."

I decided to drop it. I'd spent the day not knowing where I was going and it had all worked out fine. There was no reason not to trust the evening too. I started telling James about my day. I felt like loads had happened. It was only once I started talking that I realised I didn't really have any story to tell. My words trickled off tamely.

"Sorry, that wasn't much of a story," I said.

"Well, sounds better than my day," James said. "I'm telling you, every time I come back here they seem to have dug out some more family of mine. I know it sounds horrible but they're all the same to me. I just don't have the time to get to know any of them individually. Everyone I meet is just some other Macleod. Most of them have never left the island.

They all live in the same place. There's nothing about them that helps me remember who they are."

It was pretty dark. The radio began to cut in and out as James steered us around the tight bends in the road. He told me to look in the glove compartment for any CDs in there. I found Dark Side of the Moon and a Radiohead Best Of.

"Your dad has a decent taste in music," I said.

"I seriously doubt that."

I put on Pink Floyd. After about a minute or so I realised it was the last thing I wanted to be listening to driving out into the darkness. Too heavy. It just didn't have any adventure to it. I took the CD out and looked back in the glove compartment again. Radiohead was probably even less suitable than Pink Floyd. Under Radiohead I spotted an album cover I'd seen in pretty much every house I'd ever set foot in.

"Hey. Bob Marley. That'll do," I said. I wasn't sure I'd ever actually listened to Bob Marley before. It was just one of those things you'd always heard around.

"My mum must've left that in there. She goes through these phases where it's all she listens to. You hear her singing along while she's cooking sometimes," James said.

I couldn't really see anything out the windows by this point. It didn't matter. The music and the sound of the engine was enough for me. I didn't need the rest of my senses. Could You Be Loved felt like the only thing in the world. When it finished I jumped back to the beginning of the song. James didn't say anything.

By the time Buffalo Soldier started James was reversing

us into a spot. I couldn't really tell where we were. We didn't seem to be near anything in particular.

James grabbed the torch and the paper from my lap. He looked at the sheet for a minute. Then he got out of the car and looked around.

"Just wait here a sec. I think I know where we're going. There's no point us carrying anything until I know for sure though," he said.

A minute or two later he was back. "Alright, we're good. This is it."

"Where'd you go?" I asked.

"See that house down there? They actually built where we're staying tonight. I just went to knock on their door to check it was alright with them."

"They didn't know we were coming?" I asked.

"Nope."

"They don't mind people just turning up?"

"Nah. It's why they built it. They wanted something people could enjoy."

He lifted the bag onto his back. I knew those camping bags were designed to spread the weight out a bit so I didn't feel too guilty.

I grabbed the string bag with the firewood in and carried the torch in my free hand. James had checked the piece of paper and decided he'd lead. This meant it was my job to aim the torch ahead and follow him like a spotlight so he could see where he was walking.

We weren't actually in a car park. We'd pulled over at

the side of the road and squeezed up next to a small shed. We walked about twenty metres back up the road and climbed over a stile into a field.

"It might be wet here. I don't think there's a proper path. If you're not too cold we'll just walk slowly so we don't fall over," James said.

"No problem."

There was a wire fence about five yards to our left. I could hear James saying things out loud to himself as he walked. It sounded like he was reciting the directions so he wouldn't forget them. I didn't interrupt him. Getting lost in the darkness didn't appeal.

James was looking down at his feet and then at the fence to our left. The ground was sloping slightly to the side and in the dark it made it difficult to walk confidently. The wiry handle of the sack of wood was digging into my hand. I couldn't really complain though. James was definitely carrying the more weight.

After what felt like thirty minutes but was probably nearer two, the fence to our left began to curve round in front of us. We followed it. After another minute or two we came to another stile. James turned to me.

"Right. This is where we climb over. Then the map says it's just to the right a bit the other side. I'm not sure how far it is, I'm hoping it's obvious once we're there."

The ground was sturdier the other side of the fence. It was stonier. It was easier to stand on but still tricky to move across in the dark. My toe kept clipping upturned stones and throwing my balance off a little. I could hear the sea.

"This way," James said.

I tried to follow his feet with the torch. He was getting lower. There did seem to be a kind of path now. Not a path made for people but still a path of sorts. Each step was only about twenty centimetres further down than the previous but carrying the wood meant I had to concentrate on each step intently. At the bottom I noticed a few flowers surviving amongst the rocks.

I could hear the sea clearly now. It was loud without sounding violent. I couldn't hear James calling back to me. Eventually I caught him up and his words made it through.

"It's just round this way," he said, signaling with his right hand.

The stones were getting bigger under foot. By now they were much larger than my boots. Rather than trying to find the gaps between them I started moving from the top of one stone to another. It was a little easier and much more enjoyable.

"This is it," James said.

I shone the torch at him and then across to where he was pointing. Somehow I hadn't spotted it yet. There was a sheet of stone with a thin piece of glass in it. As we got closer I could see it was a roof. A skylight. It was like a little house.

"This is the bothy," James said.

It backed into the side of the cliff. In front was a stretch of about twenty metres. Then there was the drop. I put down the wood and walked over to the edge. I couldn't even see to the bottom of the cliff. I could only hear the sea. It must have been a straight drop of over a hundred metres.

Then there was the water. The endless water. The moonlight helped me sketch the surroundings in my mind. To our right was a strange, dramatic rock formation standing out in the ocean. Apart from that, I could make out nothing but water. It wasn't coastline. I didn't know what it was. It was unbelievable. It was so alien to me I felt something similar to fear. I couldn't process it.

"Let's get set up inside first," James said.

Around one side of the bothy was a small wooden door. Aside from the skylight and a small window, it was the only sign of any kind that this was a deliberate structure. If James hadn't known it was there I'd have walked straight past it. Straight off the edge.

James opened the door. I followed him in. It was incredible. The walls were made up of small, jagged stones from the cliff itself. There were wooden beams around the top presumably holding the roof in place. There was a small fireplace in the opposite corner and a wooden bench raised up off the floor. Through the window you could see sea and only sea. James took off the bag and placed it on the bench. I put down the wood by the fireplace.

CHAPTER 18

JAMES HAD PLANNED BETTER FOR THE NIGHT THAN I HAD FOR THE WHOLE WEEK. A crate of beer. The wood for the fire. Sleeping bags. Roll mats. A pan. Sausages. Bread. Water. Even a little speaker with a wire to connect to his phone for music.

He put on Little Richard while we unpacked. I imagined James was the first person ever to play Little Richard in the bothy. It was an odd choice but it worked. I spread out the roll-mats to work out where we'd sleep. One of us would be up on the bench and the other would be on the floor. They both had their benefits. Whoever was on the floor would be near the fire and whoever wasn't on the floor didn't have to be on the floor. I left the sleeping bags in their sacks to save space for the time being.

The walls didn't look sturdy at all. Rocks of various sizes had been wedged together and somehow it made a solid upright structure. It felt more organic than camping even though it kept the weather out far better than any tent ever could.

James dug around in the bag and pulled out a Swiss Army knife.

"This'll work hopefully. I think what we need to do is peel little flaps off the wood. That way we can light each of those and they'll burn down into the rest of the wood."

I didn't know enough to offer any more insight. James had been in the Cubs as a kid. I figured that made him more qualified than me.

James opened a beer and I took a sip from one of the water bottles. He placed a few chunks of wood in the fireplace. He picked up a piece and began going at it with the knife. The combination of beer and knife made me uneasy. He was holding the wood in his left hand. The knife, in his right, was moving along the edge of the wood straight towards his chest. It didn't look too controlled.

"At least do that away from yourself," I said.

He began moving the knife in the other direction.

"Happy?" he asked.

I watched. I didn't really know how it was meant to go.

"If you think it's fine then I'm sure it'll work," I said.

"I wouldn't rely on that logic if I were you," James replied.

He did a couple more pieces in the same way and placed them on top of the pile of wood in the fireplace. He reached into one of the pockets of the bag and pulled out a box of matches.

"For someone who can't work out that they shouldn't plunge a knife towards their own chest you're pretty well prepared," I said.

"I like to think if I prepare well enough then I don't have to pay any attention to what I'm doing."

I laughed. It was a pretty accurate assessment of his approach to life.

He crouched in front of the fire and lit a match. He moved it around the various flaps he'd made in the wood. Most stayed lit. We both watched them burn down. When one of the larger pieces caught the flames James stood up. He went over to the speaker and turned the music up. Lucille.

"Cheers!" he said, raising his beer. I tapped my water against his can.

"This might be the coolest place I've ever slept," I said.

"Might be? Stayed somewhere better in Manchester did you? Or is Essex doing a good line in bothies at the moment?" James said.

"Yeah, they've just opened a bunch around Stansted Airport actually."

The fire was growing. We decided to step outside while it heated up. We stayed around ten metres from the edge. It sloped down slightly before the drop. Neither of us were brave enough to step towards the edge just yet.

"It's kind of scary not being able to see where the bottom is," I said. "It's hard to know how high up we are."

James bent down and picked up a stone. He took a few steps forward and threw it over the edge. One of his feet gave way a little as he threw. He had to put his hand down to stop himself from falling. A second or two later we heard a splash in the water. It sounded like it came from miles away.

"Jesus," I said.

"I need to find a bigger one. Imagine how loud it'll be," James said, excited.

"There definitely isn't a beach down there is there?" I asked, realising James could be squashing midnight ramblers with his throws.

"Nah. It's just a straight drop down to the water. I'm not an idiot."

He bent down and picked up a stone that was heavy enough to require using both his hands. He started moving towards the edge.

"Hey, not-an-idiot, you slipped over throwing that tiny one a minute ago, maybe don't go right to the edge with that massive one," I said.

"Ok Mum, I won't."

He stopped around five feet short of the edge. He squatted, swung his arms back between his legs and hurled the stone forward. It clipped the edge of the cliff, bounced up and went down. A second or two later we heard the sound. It didn't sound watery. It sounded heavy. A great punch as it crashed into the sea. James laughed. I noticed the beer he'd left on the ground. I made a mental note to not let him try that again after a few more beers.

CHAPTER 19

BACK INSIDE I INSPECTED THE BOTHY SOME MORE. It was hard to see how it was still standing. Every day it got blasted by these ruthless ocean winds.

I sat on the bench and looked at the wooden beam above my head. There was a clear plastic box balancing on top. I reached up and pulled it down.

The sticker on the box read Please Leave Everything As You Found It. I opened it up. There was a book of Philip Larkin poems. It didn't seem the time to read but it was a pleasant surprise anyway. Underneath the book were around ten sheets of paper stapled together. I flicked through them.

It was a photo history of the making of the bothy. They'd started it in the nineties. There was a picture of the spot before the bothy. All the stones lying around. Then there was a suggestion of a front wall. Then there were the wooden beams sticking out of the back wall. Then there were the finished walls with the gaps for the window. Finally, there was the completed bothy, fully equipped with window, skylight and door. It was surreal seeing it come together out of nowhere. Going by the last photo, it hadn't changed a bit since it was built.

At the bottom of the last page was a small sentence in italics.

In memory of our brave daughter

"Did someone die here?" I asked.

"I don't think so. Why?"

"Look here," I said, showing James the page.

"Actually, I think I kind of know the story. I think my dad told me once. There was this woman. She grew up here and became a journalist. She went all round the world. She got killed in the Gulf war or something like that and her family wanted to build something in her memory that people could enjoy. That's why this is just here and free to use. I think that's it anyway. I'm not sure that anyone can just turn up. Well, it's not like you'd find it if you didn't know it was here anyway. I mean, I don't think they advertise it. I think it's like an open secret. They told people they trusted, who told people they trusted and so on. The woman who lives at that house we parked by, she was in and out of hospital for a while and told my mum about it. My mum and dad came out here at some point but they didn't stay. They just wanted to see it. Mum told me whenever I was next up that I had to come out here. She told the woman her son wanted to come here and she said it was fine. So here we are."

"So they know I'm here too?" I asked.

"Well, it's not like they know who you are. They've never met you. But yeah, I left a note by their door. They weren't in but I figured it's polite to leave a note. Just in case they were coming here later tonight or something. I wouldn't want them to get here and for us to scare the shit out of them."

"I don't think I've ever heard of anything like this. Anywhere."

"Yeah. It's not too bad, is it?"

I quickly flicked through the Philip Larkin book then put everything carefully back in the box. I placed the closed box back up on the beam. I moved nearer the fire. It was warming up nicely.

"Take a seat, sir. You are my guest here at this … place … bothy … and I shall feed you," James said.

"If you insist."

Anywhere else I guess it wouldn't have been much. There, that night, it felt like the greatest meal in the world.

Mary had had an excess of beef sausages from the butchers and insisted James bring them. He put them in the pan on top of the fireplace. I wasn't sure it would work but they started sizzling pretty much right away. James laid out two sets of two slices of bread and put a bottle of ketchup in the middle. After a few minutes he cut open the sausages to check they were cooked. Satisfied, he served up my sandwich first. It was fantastic. I'd finished by the time James had taken a bite.

"Thanks for that. It was so good," I said.

"No problem. There's more sausages in the bag if you fancy some more."

"I'm good for now. We can always do more later though," I said.

"Exactly. Besides, I've got something else for us to try first."

He finished off his sandwich and started rummaging through the bag again. He pulled out a pack of wooden skewers, some chocolate and a pack of marshmallows.

"You're a genius," I said.

"I believe that is the general consensus. Let's see how this goes first though."

In theory it was perfect. Skewer the marshmallows. Put a tiny piece of chocolate on. Roast the marshmallow while the chocolate melted over the top. Of course, the problem was the skewers. They began burning the second we placed them over the fire. If we held the skewers high out of the flames, the chocolate didn't melt.

"I wanted toasted marshmallows, not slightly warm marshmallows," James said. The anger in his voice amused me.

James attempted it one more time. It didn't go any better. He chucked the skewers down in disgust and started looking around. He reached behind to where he'd put the fork that'd been used for moving the sausages around the pan. Then he picked up the water bottle, poured a little over the prongs of the fork and wiped it off on his trouser leg.

"Good as new," he said.

He picked out a fresh marshmallow and pierced it with the fork. I watched as he placed a piece of chocolate on the top and put it into the flames. The marshmallow changed colour in seconds. He moved the fork quickly into his mouth, pulled a strained face and swallowed. Then he grabbed the water bottle and gulped a load down.

"Right," he said, "it's hotter than the sun, but it's better. I think I burned that one a bit. It tasted a bit charred. I'm nearly there though. I reckon if we just put the fork over and turn it round for a few seconds it'll be perfect."

James tried out his new method. The chocolate fell into the flames as he tried to rotate the marshmallow. He moved the fork to his mouth anyway.

"Perfect marshmallow at least," he said, smiling.

He handed the fork to me. I nailed it first time. The key was to move the marshmallow up and down while you waited for the chocolate to melt. It was heaven. Sickening heaven. I needed water but I wanted another one straight away.

We took turns. We didn't even really need to speak. We'd watch each other as we each tried to come up with our own perfect formula. Every now and then one of us would burn our mouths or our hands or everything would fall off the fork into the fire and we'd burst out laughing.

"Are we running low yet?" I asked.

James inspected the bag. "Still a few left actually."

"I think I'm going to be sick if I keep going," I said.

"Thank God you said that. Me too. I just couldn't stop. Every time I had one I felt like that had to be the last one. Then I'd see you have one and I'd get jealous and want another one."

We agreed on a truce. We both had one more and then we stopped.

Lucille was playing. I wondered how many times the album had looped round. Neither of us had noticed. I reached for the phone. Gaslight Anthem. That'd do.

"It'll be weird when you're working in London. You'll be sitting in your office knowing all this is out there," I said.

"Yeah. Although I did know all this was out here already. It's not like I did all that work and got this job and then suddenly found out there are bits of the world that aren't offices."

"Won't you find it hard to take it seriously though? I mean, how much do you really care about what you'll be doing?"

I felt like there was some secret James knew about that I didn't. I couldn't understand how he managed to commit to things that deep down I knew he didn't care about.

"I guess I care about it because I decided to do it. There'd be no point me getting a degree if I wasn't going to do anything with it. There'd be no point me doing this job if I didn't try and get something out of it."

"That makes sense."

"Besides, you know, most people work, pretty much everyone works. You have to work. And how many people really like their jobs? Not many. I always knew I'd have to work so I worked out what I could do and what would be good for me to do. I know it's not going to be fun."

"Some people like their jobs. Isobel loves her job," I said.

"I'm sure she does. She's one of the few. Most people don't. It's not like because you didn't train for your job that makes it better. You still don't like it. It doesn't take you any closer to where you want to be. It's not like not pulling in the wrong direction is a step in the right direction, you know?"

"Yeah, you're right. I guess I just always felt like work was something I had to do. But not a main thing. It was a side thing. Something I just happened to do because I had to. I always thought like, right, I've got this book and I've got Kim. That's what I've got going on."

"Right. But that's the point. You just had these safety nets to stop you from trying. Really trying. You weren't happy with Kim but it didn't bother you because you were fine with things being ok. It's not like you'd spend all day writing your book and really committed to that either. I just...sorry, that sounds like I'm criticising you-"

"No, no. I know what you mean. You're right. It's not like I quit my job in the name of doing what I wanted to do. If I really wanted to do it then I've no excuse for not doing it. What was stopping me? I've not given it everything, not even close. I guess I just put all my energy into Kim. Things weren't good, of course they weren't, but I'd put a lot of time into it so I guess I felt like if I could save it then it'd justify all the work I'd put in."

"Exactly. At least with work, I don't take it so personally. I can put the effort in towards these specific goals. I get a degree or I don't. I get a job or I don't. I get a pay rise or I don't. It's nothing to do with my happiness. It's just goals. I can care about it the amount I need to care about it because I know exactly what it means."

"See, I've never had that. I think I always felt like I

shouldn't try new things if I wasn't certain that they'd pay off. I already had this big, massive part of my life I knew wasn't working. I just put more and more effort into it so that when it inevitably failed I could say it wasn't my fault."

James took a sip of his beer and smiled.

"Right. I've been meaning to say this for a while," he started. "I think you're finally ready to take this the right way. How mental is it that you were going to propose to Kim? I mean, really. What would you have done if she'd said yes? You guys would've actually got married. That would be your life."

"Yeah. I guess I would've just gone along with it as long as it lasted. You're right. It is pretty ridiculous."

We both laughed.

"Just promise me something, make sure you don't make you and Kim breaking up your new thing. Don't let your life revolve around that now instead. Don't replace trying to save a bad relationship with feeling bad about a bad relationship not working out. It's a good thing. You can do whatever now. You don't have to get a job in the city or anything. But you don't have that in reserve either now. You're not waiting around for someone else to marry you. You're in charge. You have to take charge."

"That's a scary thought. I don't trust me so much," I said.

"Well, I wouldn't trust me either. I don't know anything. I've had a few beers and for all we know in a few months I'll be calling you from London saying 'Alex I was wrong let's go live in the bothy'."

"I wonder if you stayed up here long enough, whether London would seem crazy noisy. I wonder if that's why people from here never move anywhere else. They get too used to it and can't take anything else."

"Maybe," James said. "That sounds a bit sad. I guess there's nothing wrong with being content though."

"Yeah, I guess. But there's more to life than that," I said. "Nobody ever says 'he was a content man' at someone's funeral."

"Yeah, but then what about everyone else? They spend half their lives working and saving to be able to have their own content, peaceful life. What's wrong with jumping straight into that?"

"That's a good point. I guess we don't really know what it's like coming from here anyway. Your parents aren't exactly the average islanders."

"I don't know. We've been here for a few days now. I think that's enough time to completely understand the complexities of an area and its people."

CHAPTER 20

WE WENT AND SAT OUTSIDE FOR A WHILE. At one point James wandered towards the edge. He stood still for a second staring silently into the darkness. I was relieved when he turned back and sat down beside me again. I didn't want to have to tell him to come back from the edge. There's a fine line between caring and patronising and I wasn't sure I was smart enough to get it right.

The sound of the sea was hypnotic. Grand. Elegant. It was everywhere. It had this considerate beauty. You could take it in at your own pace. It didn't drown out the conversation.

At one point James told me that the next piece of land in front of us was America. It was hard to get my head round. I thought about walking through the water. I thought about all the creatures I'd see before I came across another human being.

We decided to head back inside when it started to rain. As I reached the door of the bothy I heard a big splash in the water behind me. I turned round to see James jogging back from the edge. He opened his hands in front of his chest in a 'What? Me?' pose.

James tended to the fire while I set up sleeping

arrangements. James said he wanted to keep an eye on the fire through the night so I took the bench. It was nearer the door but the fire had warmed up the entire bothy by that point so I didn't mind. Besides, I liked being raised up from the floor. I positioned myself with my head directly beneath the skylight.

James unrolled his sleeping bag and climbed in. He left one arm sticking out the top which he used to prod wood around the fireplace. I didn't know if he was actually having any effect on the fire but he looked like he had a specific aim in mind so I left him to it.

I'd left on all my clothes except for my now damp jacket. With the fire and the thick sleeping bag I was starting to sweat. I knew I couldn't take off any layers though. The fire wasn't going to last all night and I didn't want to wake up freezing.

"I've no idea what time it is," James said.

"Check my phone if you want. It's just above your head," I told him.

"Nah. I like not knowing. I don't feel any pressure to fall asleep."

I kept my eyes open. James was moving the wood less and less. He wasn't speaking much anymore either. At one point I thought I heard him snoring and assumed he'd fallen asleep. A few minutes later he rolled over and re-arranged the wood once more.

The light of the stars kept my eyes bright, so the bothy never felt dark. The stars weren't like candles. They didn't flicker. They were constant and I was grateful for them. From what I remembered of school, they might not actually exist anymore. I didn't want to close my eyes. I didn't want to miss them. My body felt completely asleep but my eyes wouldn't give in. I lay back with my hands behind my head.

Morning arrived and the stars were gone. I hadn't seen them leave. I didn't think I'd fallen asleep but maybe I had. All I knew was that the sky was moving back to lighter blues. The sea sounded different with the new sky. At night it had been relaxing. In the morning it was like the waves were charging in, ordering me to get up and start the day.

I sat up. James was still asleep. I put on my jacket, now dry, and headed outside, closing the door quietly behind me. It wasn't raining anymore. I sat down on a rock and watched the sea to the right of where we'd slept. There was a small cove where the waves rushed in, swirled around and crashed enthusiastically back into the sea.

CHAPTER 21

I FELT AWAKE. The clean air was doing something to me. I wasn't hyper or particularly energised, I just felt awake. My mind was working. My thoughts weren't cluttered. I listened to myself breathe.

James walked up behind me. "Morning. Not a bad view."

"Not bad service," I said, eyeing the sausage sandwiches he'd brought out with him. He handed me the one in his left hand and took a bite out of the other.

We shared a large stone a few metres back from the edge of the cliff. I pointed to some birds swooping down on the water. James cared more about his sausages. He didn't speak to me until he'd finished eating.

"I don't feel like I had a single drop of alcohol last night," he said.

"Me neither."

"How funny. I'm just saying, there must be something about the sea air that does it. I feel really awake. Or maybe it's this magnificent breakfast I've cooked up for us."

"I actually know what you mean. I don't feel like I slept at all but I still feel great."

James stood up and stretched his arms over his head.

"Let's wander down the cliff a bit while it's bright. See what's down there."

"As long as by down the cliff you mean-"

"- Obviously I don't mean climbing down the cliff face. I mean let's see how far along we can walk."

Having walked to the bothy in the dark, we didn't really have any idea of our surroundings. We'd walked through the fields to the back. That was all we knew. We didn't know how far the cliffs carried on either side.

In the light it was a bit easier to walk. I hopped from stone to stone while James marched ahead confidently. His ankles seemed far more flexible than mine. We didn't talk while we walked. James was staring out to sea and I was watching my feet to make sure I stayed upright.

The ground became grassier the further we walked. The rain from the night before made some patches a bit slippery.

We could see a drop ahead of us. The cliff seemed to curve round and in. James ran ahead. I walked, wary of the muddy ground.

"Holy shit!" James shouted back.

We were standing at the tip of a deep cove where the sea had worn into the cliff. There was a small beach at the bottom. The drop was sheer and steep. I eyed the cliff face, wondering if anyone could manage to climb down. I thought about how satisfying it would be to reach the beach, knowing you were the first person to set foot there.

The water rushed in and covered the beach. As it rushed out again I noticed a small cave at one side of the sand. It looked small from where we were but was likely big enough for someone to walk into without ducking. The mouth of the cave was frothing from where the water had been. Every few seconds it filled up and then emptied again. The new froth was dragged around by the force of the waves.

"It's a shame kids probably never get out here," I said. "It looks like somewhere a monster could live. I'd have loved this as a kid."

Even the cave looked like the mouth of a mad monster, guzzling up the sea and spitting it out again.

"Look," said James.

He was pointing back out towards the sea. There must have been over two hundred birds diving and bombing into the water. It was a manic scene. You could hear the howls of the birds. They sounded ecstatic and frustrated. I guess no matter how many fish there are it's never enough.

"I think they're gannets," James said.

That made sense. Growing up my mum had always used the word gannet when we'd been eating. I'd never really thought about what it meant. I hadn't connected it to the bird. My mum had used it from such a young age that the word gannet was imprinted on my brain as someone who is eating greedily. For me, that was the context and the meaning of the word. I didn't admit to James I'd only just realised what a gannet was. It had taken him about two years to drop it when I let slip that I thought ponies were baby horses.

We watched the waves and the birds and the clouds all moving in their own ways. It was stunning. It made me feel something close to sadness. I wasn't sure why. Maybe it was the thought that back in the real world none of this made a difference.

It was my turn to drive us back. James had driven in the dark so I definitely got the better part of the deal. Carrying our stuff back to the car was easier too. There was no wood to carry. The food had been eaten and the drinks had been drunk. I carried the bag this time, a token gesture given that it must've been twice as heavy the night before.

Walking back to the car, James kept talking about how awake he felt. He said he felt like everyone should have to spend at least one night a year somewhere like that, doing what we'd just done.

Five minutes into the drive back I could hear James snoring in the seat next to me. I put Bob Marley on again.

CHAPTER 22

THE RAIN HELD OFF FOR MOST OF THE DRIVE BACK. As we pulled into Keose it really started coming down. The noise of the water slapping against the windscreen woke James up.

"You're so awake this morning aren't you?" I said.

"Shut up. It's being stuck in a car with you that puts me to sleep." He yawned dramatically.

It wasn't even ten yet. It threw me a little. My body felt good but it did feel late in the day. James told me he was going to go straight to bed. There was nobody else around when we got in so I wasn't sure what to do.

I went upstairs to my room. I tried to read but my mind kept wandering. It wasn't long until I fell asleep.

I woke up to the sound of the house under attack. The rain was banging madly on the window. I could hear things moving around outside in the wind.

Downstairs I found Mary where I always found her.

"How was your night?" she asked.

"Good. Yeah, really good. I don't know what I expected but not that…I'm really pleased we went."

"That's nice. I thought you two would like it. The weather wasn't too bad was it?"

"It was fine. It was worth the rain anyway."

"Well, it took it out of that son of mine, that's for sure. He's been asleep all day."

"He's still asleep?" I asked.

"Yep. He didn't move a muscle when I went in to see him. Dead to the world."

"That's funny. All morning he kept telling me how awake he felt. Then he fell asleep the minute we got in the car."

"That sounds about right. Now, I don't know what you want to do with yourself, Alex. The weather isn't exactly great for going outside."

"I'll be fine, Mary. You don't have to entertain me every minute of the day."

"I know. I know you can take care of yourself. I'd just hate for you to feel bored while you're here."

"I couldn't feel like that here. Honestly Mary, you don't have to worry. I'll go upstairs and read for a bit. If I get that bored I'll go in and give James a kick."

"I'll be getting him up in an hour or two anyway" she said. "He's having dinner with us whether he likes it or not."

CHAPTER 23

I HADN'T BROUGHT MY LAPTOP WITH ME. Deliberately. I didn't want to get stuck in the cycle of checking emails, forums and everything while I was away. It was usually my main source of entertainment. Watching things or clicking around aimlessly or even doing my writing. It all happened on my laptop.

It was a shame. I was actually in the mood for writing. The rest of my book was hundreds of miles away and for once I had the urge to get some writing done. I decided to forget the mystery book. It was a hassle. Maybe the reason I never felt inspired was because it wasn't inspiring enough.

I went downstairs and asked Mary if she had a pad I could use. She couldn't find one so she took a chunk of paper out of the printer for me. I thanked her, grabbed a pencil and headed back upstairs.

I sat on the floor and started writing. More scribbling really. It was barely legible. I didn't stop to think about what to put next. My hand just kept going across the page.

I knew nothing would come of it but that relaxed me. I wasn't thinking about the kids on the playground trying to work it out. I wasn't imagining my mum reading it. I just let the pencil do the work. Of course, it was no good. But it was fun.

It was a story. About an old guy called Trevor. Trevor lived alone. He had this rat called Juniper. He'd had rats his whole life and each one was called Juniper. It had gone on for so long he couldn't even remember where the name Juniper had come from. Each time he found the rat had passed away he'd get a replacement and carry on as normal.

Trevor had lived for so long and found life so lonely that he couldn't recognise good things when they happened. Late in life a string of brilliant things happened to him. He saw each off with a shrug. He would always say "Is this the way life is, Juniper?" and the latest Juniper would stare back at him blankly.

A beautiful neighbour began to seek his company. Is this the way life is, Juniper? A forgotten acquaintance leaves him a great deal of money. Is this the way life is, Juniper?

I wasn't sure what it meant or if it meant anything at all. I don't think it really made sense. I was unclogged though. That was something. It didn't matter if it was good. Sometimes you have to throw up to get the poison out. It doesn't mean it tastes good when you do it.

The lead on the pencil started to wear away. Writing with a blunt pencil gave me shivers. Something about the sensation of it scraping across the paper made my whole body tense. It was distracting. I knew I'd have to stop soon.

James made me jump. He was standing in the doorway

in his boxers, stretching. He hadn't said a word. He let out a
huge yawn.

"I think Mum wants us for dinner," he said.

CHAPTER 24

IT WASN'T A ROAST THIS TIME. It wasn't any less extravagant though. Mary seemed to exclusively serve feasts. They weren't fancy. She wasn't showing off. She just seemed to love feeding people.

Mary let us tuck in for a few minutes before she delivered her ultimatum.

"Now, you two, you're going to stay downstairs this evening. It's only a few days until you leave and I feel like we've hardly seen each other."

"I feel like we've been here ages," I said. "I mean … in a good way."

"Well, tonight it might feel like you're sitting downstairs with us for ages. And not in a good way. But I don't care. That's a mum's right. I've not seen my son in ages," Mary said.

"I'm right here Mum," James said, waving.

"Very funny," said Martin, his mouth full, "you'll do what your mother says."

James had sent Martin the DVD of Into The Wild for his birthday a couple of months back. Martin hadn't watched it. James knew he wasn't going to either. James said Martin never wanted anything for his birthday so he always had to choose something at random. He said he'd always find the presents he'd sent lying around the house unused. Unopened DVDs or unread books sitting in some corner gathering dust. It had happened enough times now that James didn't take it personally. He'd thought Martin might like this one though. When Martin was in his twenties he'd driven across America. James thought maybe the film might bring back some memories for him.

After dinner we all settled in the living room to watch the film. Only James had seen it before. I'd heard the soundtrack and really liked it but never got around to actually watching the film.

I loved it. I thought it was great. Some of the shots were beautiful. I felt satisfied to be watching it somewhere equally stunning and unusual. The fact that I already loved the soundtrack probably seduced me a little. A pretty landscape with a great song is a hard thing to resist. I didn't even find the ending sad. At least he'd done it. At least he was out there. He wasn't stuck at home, saving money for something he didn't even want. He went straight where he wanted to be. He saw exactly what he wanted to see.

Martin hated it. I mean, he really hated it. He stayed silent for most of the film but by the end he couldn't hold it in anymore.

"This guy's an idiot!" he shouted. "Are we meant to feel sorry for him because he's stupid? Of course he was going to die."

James laughed. Mary was a little shocked. She'd teared up

at the end. She reminded Martin that they had a son roughly the same age as the guy in the film.

"As foolish as my son can be he'd never do something as idiotic as that," Martin said.

A big discussion followed. Nobody really had a side in it apart from Martin. He was set in his declaration that the guy was an idiot. Mary kept insisting it wasn't right that he felt no sympathy for the death of a young man.

Martin asked me what I thought. I told him I liked the film. He asked why. I said I liked the soundtrack. I said I liked the way it was shot. I told him I kind of liked the idea of moving from place to place, doing whatever you like. I said I thought it was kind of inspiring.

"Inspiring? What about the ending? What about his lack of planning? What about how selfish he was? What about the fact that he basically killed himself through pig-headed stupidity?"

I told him I wasn't as bothered about that. I admitted I was kind of ignoring the ending to justify enjoying the start.

"You didn't find the story inspiring," Martin said. "You liked the music and the views and the idea of meeting people. That's fine. Those things are inspiring and you can do those things. You don't have to kill yourself over it. You should stay alive and do more of those things. Even that guy realised at the end that it was all pointless without anyone to share it with. He's no hero. He was wrong. He's an idiot."

I couldn't disagree with anything Martin was saying.

"They shouldn't glorify that guy," Martin said finally,

drawing the discussion to a close. He got out of his chair and headed to the kitchen.

"I've never seen Dad react like that before," James said.

"It wasn't the film," Mary said. "I think it's because it's a true story. That's what's annoyed him. When your dad went across America, he was with two other guys. When your dad and one of them decided to come home, the other guy stayed out there. Steve, his name was. He said he didn't need a car, he'd just hitchhike around. They had this big argument about it. Your dad thought it wasn't safe. Steve told him he wasn't romantic enough. He said your dad was going back to a boring office life while Steve would still be out there, having these adventures.

For a few months your dad got these postcards from Steve. Pictures of deserts and mountains and places like that. Deliberately these beautiful landscapes. They'd always say 'how's work?' or something on the back. It would drive your dad crazy. Then the postcards stopped. Eventually, word reached your dad that Steve had been attacked. He was hitchhiking and got picked up by some guys who ended up robbing him. They beat him and left him at the side of the road.

He didn't know anyone out there, not really, and he didn't have any money. He got himself to hospital and got stitched up. Then he came back to England. He had this big scar across his face and one of his eyes wouldn't open properly. The cut went from his forehead, across his eye, down his cheek. Your dad only heard about it through someone who'd seen Steve in a pub somewhere. He tried to arrange to meet him but Steve just ignored him. I guess maybe he was too proud. Or too ashamed. I don't really know. Your dad's always been hurt by the whole thing. He's always wanted to tell Steve he's not mad at him and hopes he's ok. I guess that's why the film upset him so much. That boy's family never got the chance to tell him anything. He went off and never came back."

I didn't know what to say. Apparently, neither did James.

"Nothing to worry about," Mary carried on cheerily, "I just didn't want the pair of you thinking he'd over-reacted for no reason. For what it's worth, I quite liked the film. It's sad that the boy was so lonely but some of the scenery was very pretty."

I felt like, with that simple thought, Mary had probably got the film better than the rest of us.

CHAPTER 25

IT WAS WEDNESDAY MORNING. We were leaving on Friday. There was only one full day before I had to head back to my uneventful, uncertain life.

The sky was back to a bright blue. It made me think that maybe there was a conspiracy on the islands to make sure nobody on the mainland found out that the weather isn't as bad as they think. I'd prepared for a week of storms and darkness and mainly seen anything but. It was cold, sure, but that's tolerable as long as it's bright.

Mary was in the kitchen working on a list. She was worrying about how much stuff they needed to get for the party the next night. It was Martin and Mary's thirtieth anniversary. It was strange for me to think that for every moment of my life they'd been married. When I said my first word, they were married. When I first went to school, they were married. When I played football or drank beer or met Kim, they were married. And here they were. Still married. Still happy. Still great. It was humbling.

James and I had to work pretty hard to make Mary cave and agree to us doing the shop for her. She handed us the completed list and gave James one of her credit cards. The notion that James and I could foot the bill was a step too far for Mary.

"I'll be checking my bank balance to make sure you use that card and not yours," Mary said as we left.

James drove. Island FM was the same as always. Taylor Swift. Nirvana. M People.

Parking at Tesco was a nightmare. The car park was nowhere near big enough. Especially given that pretty much everyone on the island was relying on Tesco for their food.

Inside it wasn't much better. The aisles were blocked with trolleys. People were stopping every few metres for a chat. I guessed everyone knew each other and couldn't be seen to ignore anyone. They had to stop and catch up. Otherwise word would get round. So and so ignored so and so in Tesco the other day. Scandal. I wondered if some people came in early in the mornings just to avoid their conversational duties.

We managed to get through the vegetable aisle before it happened to us. I recognised the face but couldn't remember the name. I'd met him on my first night at the house.

"How's your mum doing?" he asked.

"Not bad. Busy worrying about tomorrow. You know what she's like," James said.

"Aye. She's a good host your mum," the man said.

"Anyway, we're on supply duty. We've got to keep moving," James said.

"No bother. See you tomorrow."

I thanked James for keeping it brief.

"To be honest," he said, "I couldn't remember the guy's

name and wanted to get moving before he noticed."

A couple more times people tried to stop us for a chat. Well, they tried to stop James for a chat. I stood silently watching while James did his best to keep us moving. He was pretty good at getting the pleasantries over quickly. He didn't have to worry about people thinking he was rude either. He didn't live on the island. Besides, I was starting to get the feeling that Mary carried so much goodwill with everyone she knew that James was never going to be able to undo it.

I pushed the trolley while James fetched the items. Every now and then he'd ask my opinion on which jar looked more fancy or something like that. We decided not to spend too much time deliberating. If we couldn't choose we picked with our eyes closed. James figured Mary had bigger things to worry about than how accurately we'd done the shopping.

I winced when the total came to over a hundred quid. It was a lot of money. Maybe Mary hadn't meant to spend that much. I was kind of relieved I didn't have to pay it but I felt guilty that I wasn't contributing. Mary had gone out of her way to keep me well fed and I wasn't offering anything in return.

We loaded the bags into the boot of the car.

"I've been thinking, I told my dad I'd go over to Ness tomorrow to pick up his trailer. I might as well just get that done now," James said.

"That makes sense. How far is it?"

"It's pretty far. The thing is, it's closer to here than it is the house. I don't really fancy doing the drive all over again tomorrow."

"That's fine," I said.

"Actually, what I was thinking is, to save you sitting in the car, you could try and see Isobel while I drive over."

James had this knack of being generous in a way that made it seem like he didn't even realise he was being thoughtful.

"It would be good to see her before we go. I don't mind keeping you company though," I said.

"It's fine, really. It's one of my dad's mates who borrowed his trailer. I'll probably have to stop in and say hello and all that. I figured I'd spare you at least one more introduction."

"I appreciate that."

James drove us over to Isobel's place. I knocked on the door. James explained what was happening.

"…so I figured I could leave him with you," he concluded.

"No problem. Don't you worry. I'll take care of him," Isobel said, ruffling my hair.

James got back in the car and through the window told us to meet him at McNeil's in a couple of hours. I told him I didn't know where that was. He laughed.

"No shit. Isobel knows though. Not everything's about you, you know. It's in town. I'll see you there later."

Isobel waved dramatically until the car turned out of sight. We hadn't actually spoken to each other yet.

"Right," she declared, "The weather's not too bad. Let's go to the castle while it lasts."

"Yes, not bad thanks Isobel. And how are you?"

"Yeah, yeah. Hello. How are you? Blah blah blah. Great. Now let's get going while the weather lasts."

Last time we were together she'd been half asleep. Her new energy took me by surprise. Going from avoiding conversation in Tesco to a full on blast of Isobel took a bit of adjusting.

CHAPTER 26

WE WALKED PAST THE HOSPITAL. I saw a McDonalds wrapper under the seat in the bus stop outside.

"Oh, is there a McDonalds somewhere here?" I asked.

Isobel laughed.

"I know you've not been here long but surely you know the answer to that," she said.

"Well, I wouldn't have thought there was but I saw a wrapper on the floor back there."

"I guess people must buy it on the mainland and bring it on the ferry. I wouldn't know how far the nearest McDonalds is though. There's nothing like that at Ullapool."

"It's kind of sad that people want it so much they bring it over with them," I said.

"I guess. Maybe it's like people going over to France for booze. People here go over to the mainland and bring back vans full of fast food."

I laughed.

We were walking down the road James and I had driven down earlier. We didn't follow the path into town though. Instead we crossed a small wooden bridge. It took us over the water that ran down into the harbour. There were ducks floating quietly beneath us.

"I like ducks. I think they're really funny," Isobel said.

"I used to live by this pond," I said, "and there was a little decking bit where people could sit and fish or whatever. One time I saw this duck standing up on the decking quacking really loudly. All these other ducks were on the grass beneath it. When the duck finished quacking all the other ducks started quacking really loudly. It was like duck stand-up comedy. Or a duck political rally or something."

Isobel laughed. "You're an idiot," she said.

"You know, I've actually told that story so many times I don't even really remember it happening anymore. I just remember telling the story. One time I heard someone else tell a really similar story. It made me think that either ducks do that sort of thing all the time, or I overheard it somewhere and convinced myself it happened to me."

"So not only are you someone who tells duck anecdotes multiple times, the anecdote isn't even definitely something that actually happened to you. It's just duck hearsay," Isobel said.

"I guess."

"You're a fascinating man," she said, smiling.

"I am. You're lucky to have the pleasure of my company. I imagine it's like hanging out with Oscar Wilde."

"Something like that, yeah."

The other side of the bridge was peaceful. You couldn't really hear the cars in town even though the road was only about twenty metres across the water. There were these tall, nearly bare trees. A sign warned me that the trees marked the edge of a golf course.

The trees curved round to the right. We carried on straight, keeping the water to our left. I realised it was a drop of about ten feet down to the water and there wasn't a proper fence or anything. There was just a stone wall at the edge of the path that was at most two feet high. I wondered whether drunks or little kids ever fell in.

We reached a grass-covered slope. At the top stood the castle. I could see it clearly at last. The left half looked a darker brown than the right. I realised that line must mark the spot where they'd started the renovations. In total, it was smaller than I expected.

"If it weren't for the grounds, I don't think it'd be worth coming up to the castle," Isobel said. "When I first got to Lewis everyone told me to walk here and I was kind of disappointed by the castle up close. It was only when I found the rest of the grounds that I fell in love with the place."

"Yeah. It is nice here. With the water and trees and everything," I said.

"This isn't it, you know. This is just the start. We've got a lot of walking to do yet. As long as the weather stays good, I mean. There's nowhere to hide out in the grounds so it's not a good place to get caught in the rain."

"I'm happy to walk however far," I said.

"Good. It gets a lot prettier than this."

We reached a small car park. I wasn't sure why it was there. It stuck out into the water. There wasn't anything around except for a couple of picnic benches. There was one empty car facing across the water back towards town.

I thought we'd gone as far as we could walk. There were old metal gates blocking our way. There was a padlock holding the two sides together. Isobel walked to the side and pushed one of the gates at the hinge. The rusted hinge gave way and left us a gap to walk through. The gates would still stop cars but apparently on foot people could get past whenever they wanted.

It was an odd layout. The path was the width of a road. Obviously at some point cars had been allowed this way. Now though the ground was all loose stones and twigs. Right was a thick wall of bushes. Left was the drop down to the open water. The wall at the edge was still only a couple of feet high.

The path wound round a few bends. Each bend concealed where the path moved next. We were moving away from Stornoway, that was all I knew. I could see it back across the water. We were passing it by. I didn't really know the layout of the island well enough to know which direction we were heading in.

Every fifty metres or so we passed a wooden bench facing out to the water. The first lined up with Stornoway. The second with the harbour. The third with the sea.

"When I first came here I wanted to take some photos to send to people" Isobel said. "Here I didn't have to pay any attention when I did it. I just stopped every time I saw a bench and took a picture. They've put one at every spot with a good view."

"It's pretty cool that no-one makes money off it. There's just benches everywhere for people to enjoy the views."

"Yeah. It's sad to think one day they'll probably charge people to come this way."

I had no idea how far we'd walked. I didn't know where we were heading. I didn't know whether the path looped back round towards the castle or if we'd have to come back the way we came.

Even beyond the harbour, the water was perfectly still. There were a few small boats tied up, floating just out of reach. In the distance I could see a lighthouse on a stretch of land reaching out into the water. I realised that land was protecting us from the chaos of the sea. That's why the harbour had been built where it was. The chunk of land left a small opening in the water just big enough for the boats to make it through.

We passed a couple walking a little terrier. It was on a loose lead and sprinted towards us. Isobel bent down and rubbed behind his ears. The couple apologised. The dog looked like one of those old-fashioned teddy bears. I wasn't surprised when I heard the lady call the dog Teddy.

Next came a man jogging in tight lycra.

"I wish I was brave enough to go running here," Isobel said. "I get worried about being caught in the rain."

"I wish I was brave enough to go running at all," I said. "I don't think I've done any running since they made me do it at school. I know it's lazy not to."

The path took a right turn. The world seemed to change in an instant. No longer were we looking out to sea. Gone was the rough, stony path. Now the path was thin, smooth and concrete. Both sides were sheltered by thick trees. The leaves weren't any one colour. It felt like we'd walked into an old painting.

The path veered downhill and we reached a junction.

"Let's go this way," Isobel said, gesturing left. "I don't know if it's the best way to go but it's the way I came when I first got here and it made me fall in love with the place."

We followed her route and reached a point where the trees stopped. There was a giant boulder resting in a thick wall of bushes. It cast a dark shadow. For a second I was thrown back into childhood, seeing monsters in every secret crevice. I thought of the cave at the bothy. I envied the kids who grew up with this nearby.

Another thirty seconds and then we stopped again. Total silence. It was really beautiful. Simple and oddly overwhelming. There was a gap in the leafy bank to our left. Water had run in up to the path where we stood. It created a round pool of perfectly blue water. If you followed where the water came in you could see all the way back out to sea. There was nothing but water out there. There was just us, the silence and this seemingly deliberate framing of stillness. It was like the island wanted to make sure nobody could pass by without noticing how beautiful it was.

"When I saw this I got why everyone told me to come out here," Isobel said.

"Yeah. It's … I don't know what. There's something about it."

"I feel like it could be anywhere in the world. I mean, town is only over there but this feels so far away from everything else."

"Does it ever get busy round here?" I asked.

"When it's sunny you see a few more people. A lot of people walk their dogs here. It's never noisy or crowded though. You always feel like you're on your own little journey."

Isobel was sitting on a stone just at the edge of the water. I was standing behind her. We'd stopped just long enough to feel a slight chill.

"Shall we keep walking?" I said.

"Absolutely," she said, jumping up from her seat.

The path took another sharp turn. I could hear running water now. Crackling but soothing.

We were amongst trees again. This time their leaves were somewhere between a gentle brown and a bright orange. The gaps between the trees allowed us to see through to the running water. Down to the left of the path was a stream about five foot across. It was clear enough that you could see right to the bottom. There were clusters of various sized rocks sitting in the water. You could see the water fizzing in different directions as it got caught among the rocks. The further we moved upstream the larger the rocks became. At one point there was a barricade of four or five large angular rocks. The water was building up on one side and bubbling out slowly between the gaps on the other.

"Look," said Isobel, pointing. I followed her finger.

"What is it?" I asked.

There was a bird standing in the water just the other side of the rocks. It was quite tall. It had long thin legs and a brightly coloured beak. It took a couple of steps in our direction. Its legs were so thin it seemed to struggle to move in the flow of the water. It didn't seem to have noticed us.

"A heron maybe? I don't really know about birds."

"Do they have herons around here?" I asked.

"I don't know. I guess so. They should have an app where you point your phone at a bird and it tells you what bird it is," she said.

"Yeah. That would be pretty useful in this exact situation and absolutely no other time."

Isobel laughed.

We walked forward quietly and reached the point in the path adjacent to where the bird was operating. It still didn't seem bothered. Every few seconds it did a few manic, precise jabs into the water with its beak. Then it would stand still again, assessing the situation before beginning the next round of jabs.

"I don't know what to do," Isobel whispered.

I smiled. I didn't know what to do either. It felt like a shame to leave. Like wasting an opportunity. I couldn't work out what the opportunity was though. We couldn't spend the rest of our lives sitting watching a bird in a stream. Eventually Isobel tugged on my hand and we started walking again.

The stream widened out and the gushing got louder. There was something satisfying about all the noise. It was relaxing. It sounded completely different to the sea at the bothy but the effect it had on me was pretty similar.

We reached a small fenced off sort of garden area. The path looped all the way around the outside and shot off in different directions at each corner.

"Do you mind if we sit for a bit?" Isobel said. "I really like it round here."

We went through the wooden gate and found a bench in the garden. It had a plaque.

In loving memory of Angus and Mairi Macleod,
who loved this place together.

I noticed a few benches around the place. They each seemed to have one of these plaques on. I wasn't sure if it demeaned the gesture a bit to be surrounded by a bunch of other benches dedicated to a bunch of other people. I guess the tombstone of someone you love isn't any less significant just because it's in a cemetery surrounded by other tombstones.

"I wonder why they always put benches in memory of people," Isobel said. "I mean, it's weird how normal it is. I don't know how it caught on."

"I guess it's just nicer than leaving flowers at the spot where someone died. Like when you see it at the side of the road and the flowers are tied to a lamp-post and all faded and worn away. With a bench you know they haven't been forgotten. All those people who sit on the bench will enjoy the same view those people being remembered enjoyed. I mean, that's me assuming that they put benches in spots the dead person liked to visit. It wouldn't make any sense if they put the benches in random places they'd never been."

Isobel took off one of her shoes. She turned it upside down and shook it.

"I keep feeling this stone in my shoe," she said. "I can't find it though. I shook it out before when we were at that bit with the boulder. I thought it was gone but I can feel it again now. Maybe it's just these shoes. That's the problem with Primark. Everything costs three quid so you think you're getting a bargain. You don't think about how you have to go back every month to get a replacement once they fall apart."

"They just opened a massive Primark back home," I said. "It's mad. It's the only shop I've ever been in where people don't even pretend to care about the shop. They pick something up, check the size, then throw it to one side. They don't put anything back. There were t-shirts on the floor and stuff in random piles everywhere. People just push past each other trying to find the stuff that isn't all torn and stretched out of shape."

"Yeah. Primark's the best," Isobel said.

I heard rustling in the tree behind us. The branches reached out over our heads. I looked up and saw a squirrel.

"Look," I whispered. Isobel smiled.

The squirrel sat looking out over the garden. All three of us waited for something to happen. The wind moved through the bushes on the other side of the garden. The squirrel sprinted along the branch, around down the trunk of the tree and out of sight.

"Nervous chap," Isobel said.

"I guess it's hard to hang around all these plaques and not be reminded of your own mortality. He's probably just a bit on edge from the heavy vibe."

There was a small pond near the fence opposite where we were sitting. I got up and walked over. Isobel stayed on the bench, her shoe still in hand.

I peered into the water. It was perfectly clear. I could see the little pebbles sitting on the bottom. There were a few newts darting back and forth. It was hard to keep track of them. From where I was standing, the pond seemed silent and peaceful. Under the water it looked pretty hectic. The newts seemed urgent and nervy. I looked over to Isobel and smiled. She mimed not being able to see me, slowly recognising who I was, and then waving enthusiastically.

Back at the bench I told Isobel about the newts.

"Are you sure that's what they were?" she said.

"Not really."

Isobel gave her shoe one last dramatic shake and then put it back on her foot. She jumped up.

"Right," she said, "enough dilly-dallying. Let's get going."

Our pace picked up once we were walking again. Neither of us would admit it, but it was getting colder by the minute. Isobel seemed to know the grounds pretty well. Without her I would've been lost forever. The paths looped round and round and offered junctions with no indication of where either path went.

"There's one more place we've got to go," she insisted. "If

it gets darker that's not a bad thing, as long as it's not so dark we can't find our way back. In which case we'll just have to live here."

"No problem. I can't imagine there's anything scary about woods at night anyway."

Isobel obviously had a set route in mind. She wasn't pausing to make up her mind anymore.

The path began to rise. I knew we were circling a hill but the thick trees on either side of the path made it impossible to tell both where the hill was and how far we had climbed.

"Just up here," she assured me.

The trees made way for a small patch of grass. There was yet another bench. Isobel climbed up on it and stood high above me. I stayed behind her, my hands resting on the cold wood of the top of the bench. We both looked out at the view. It was Stornoway. The whole of Stornoway. I could see the ferry waiting in the water. I could see Tesco. I could see the different colours of the shops. The unmanned boats sitting in the harbour. More than that I could see past Stornoway. I could see endless green brown stretches outside town. It reminded me how isolated the place was. I wasn't even thinking about the island floating in the middle of the sea anymore. The town itself was floating in the middle of all these wild fields and hills.

I walked round a bit. I tried to get a sense of where we were. To the left was more green and brown. The only things you could make out were some power lines and a tall stone structure.

"What's that?" I asked.

"What's what?"

Isobel jumped down from the bench and came over to me. I pointed out at the stone structure.

"Oh, that's the war memorial. You can see it basically wherever you are. Sometimes at night they light it up. It looks pretty nice. I've never actually been over there. I don't think you can go up it anymore. I like that you can see it from so far away though" she said.

"It's like the Lewis Eiffel Tower," I said. "You can see it everywhere you go so you don't actually need to go see it up close."

"You should work for the tourist board."

I turned back towards Stornoway. I thought about all the people in the buildings I could see. They had no idea I was looking down over them. It made whatever they were doing seem unimportant and small. How important could any of it really be if I could see it all happening at once?

Apparently Isobel was caught up in her own thoughts.

"I wish I could fly," she said. "I want to have this view all the time. I want to be able to get closer too but still have this view. I wish I could see everyone on all the streets. Watch the top of their heads as they go about their business."

"Can you see up here from town?" I asked.

"You know, I've never actually checked. I can't imagine they'd be able to make us out. It's pretty far. They can probably see the top of the hill sticking out over the trees though."

She then gave a loud "HELLO!" and an enthusiastic wave

towards the town. It made me jump.

"You like waving, don't you?" I said.

"Who doesn't like waving?" Isobel replied.

"Fair enough."

"Let's get going. I promised James I'd take good care of you. I don't want you catching cold."

We didn't seem to re-tread any of our steps on the way back. Isobel knew exactly where to go. She told me the first time she came to the grounds it took her forever to find a way out. She said she still didn't think she'd seen every bit there was to see. That was her goal. She said she wanted to walk every bit of path there was. Her enthusiasm made me smile.

Back in front of the castle, it looked kind of artificial. It didn't seem like much compared to what was out there.

~~~~~

It was strange to be back in town so quickly. I looked at people in the windows of cafes. I didn't know why they were in there, paying over the odds for coffee and cakes. They had endless paths they could be exploring.

But I knew I was in no position to judge really. These people actually lived here. They probably had experiences like I'd just had all the time. I was the one who lived in a big grey town and never walked just for the sake of it. They probably looked across the sea to the mainland and wondered why people like me live the way we do. I didn't have a good reason.

Isobel said she'd been to McNeil's a couple of times

before. It was right in the middle of town. Next to the library and opposite the bookshop. Not a bad spot.

CHAPTER 27

JAMES WAS ALREADY IN MCNEIL'S. He was standing at the bar talking to the landlady. He turned when he heard us come in.

"This is them," he said to the woman at the bar. "Good timing," he said to Isobel and me.

"Everything sorted?" I asked.

"Yeah, I got caught in a sheep jam on the way back though. It was pretty annoying. There was this one dopey sheep that wouldn't get out of the road," he said.

"A sheep jam?" I asked.

"Yeah. This farmer was moving all his sheep down the road. They were taking up both lanes. I went slowly behind them for a bit, waiting for them to move. Then this car came the other way and they started panicking. The farmer led them off down some path. This one sheep kept going though. He moved from one lane to the other, zig-zagging. It was like he was doing it on purpose. You know how when you're in a hurry and you can't get round someone on the pavement? You go one way and it feels like they go the same way just to block you? It was like that. Only instead of a guy it was a sheep."

Isobel and I laughed.

"Fancy a drink?" James asked.

"What are you having?" I asked him.

"Ginger beer. I've still got to get this trailer back to the house in one piece."

"I'll have a white wine if that's alright," Isobel said.

"Of course."

"Just a coke would be good, cheers," I said.

James paid for the drinks and carried them over to a table in the corner. The pub was empty. It was just us and the woman at the bar. The wooden floor made our steps echo around the room. It was awkward to talk knowing the woman couldn't help but hear every word we said.

Luckily, Isobel had spotted a solution.

"Is that a jukebox over there? Any requests?"

"Whatever you deem appropriate," James said.

Isobel wandered over to the jukebox. She took a couple of minutes making her choices. She was obviously taking the responsibility seriously. While we waited I filled James in on what we'd done with the day.

Bruce Springsteen came on. Dancing In The Dark. The scene made me laugh. It was kind of surreal. James and I sitting in the corner talking. The woman at the bar cleaning glasses. The empty pub, the clear wooden floor and the sole girl in the corner, white wine in hand, happily choosing at the jukebox, dancing from one foot to the other.

The song had nearly ended by the time she sat back down.

"I chose five. Maybe it'll make you think of something you guys want to put on next. Either because you like my songs or because they'll annoy you so much you'll want to hear something else."

This Charming Man.

"I've no problem with this," James said.

I'd been avoiding The Smiths for a while. They made me think of Manchester. And everything that happened there. For some reason, at that moment they felt full of ecstasy.

"Me and James have seen Morrissey and Marr live," I said. "Separately of course, but still …"

"To be honest, I'm not really cool enough to know lots of their songs. I just know the big ones," Isobel said.

"I didn't know much when we first saw Morrissey – we just went because it was on. It was good. It made me chase down the rest of it. Even the solo stuff. So when Johnny Marr started touring solo, we went to see him too."

"I guess that's what counts. You can tell people you've seen them live and technically not be lying."

"Exactly," James said. "I saw AC/DC and Aerosmith a few years back. When I tell my kids I'll just hope they won't do the maths. They might think I saw them when they were still good."

We talked about different bands we'd seen live. Isobel had been to a few gigs when she was abroad. She said it wasn't really any different to in England. Everywhere you go there's drunk people yelling the wrong words along.

Oasis. Lyla. Unusual Oasis choice.

"I don't even really like Oasis," Isobel said. "I just panicked."

"We saw them live too," James said. "They were alright. Their fans are dickheads though."

"That surprises me, they seem like such lovely chaps," she said.

"Right, that's it. You've won me over. I'll go choose something to put on next," James said, getting up and heading over to the jukebox.

"It's funny, because it's so empty I felt under loads of pressure choosing songs. There's not any other noise to cancel out what I put on," Isobel said.

"That's silly. It's not like we're going to judge you. I'd be more scared of doing it if there were loads of people here. They might not like what I choose."

"That'd be ok though. They'd all be talking and there'd be lots of other noise. No-one would be focusing on what you chose."

"Yeah, you're probably right."

James was still making his selections. I called over to him.

"Can you put The Doors on?"

"If I have any spare spots left, I'll consider it," he replied.

T-Rex came and went. I saw the woman at the bar dancing a little. Then came Beyonce. I couldn't remember the name of the song but I knew it was Beyonce. I looked at Isobel.

"What happened to you not judging me?" she said.

"I'm not judging. Just checking it was deliberate," I said.

"Very deliberate." She tapped her glass to the music.

James sat back down and finished his drink.

"I have to say, I made some fantastic choices," he said.

"Need another drink, James?" Isobel asked.

"Maybe an orange juice and lemonade actually."

"No problem. And for you?" she said to me.

"Another coke would be good."

"Right away, sir."

Beyonce faded away and Gimme Shelter came on. There's never a bad time to hear the start of Gimme Shelter.

"I told you," James said. "All killer choices."

Isobel came back with the drinks. She'd got herself another glass of wine and a glass of water to go with it.

"Who is this?" she asked.

"The Stones," James said.

"Of course," she said, pulling a face, "I knew that."

The next song I recognised right away.

"It's been stuck in my head all day," James said.

It was Hard Sun. From the Into The Wild soundtrack. It had this distinctive jangly sort of opening.

"What is it?" Isobel asked.

"It's by Eddie Vedder. The guy from Pearl Jam. Have you ever seen Into The Wild?" I asked her.

"Is that the one about the guy who dies in the middle of nowhere?" she said.

"Yeah, I suppose it is," James said, laughing.

"It's more than that though. It's a good film," I told her. "It's about him travelling across America. I think you'd like it."

"My dad didn't like it," James said.

"How come?" Isobel asked.

"It was mad. It made him really angry. He actually

stormed out of the room at the end. My mum told us he took it a bit personally. Apparently one of his mates did something like that when he was young and got really hurt. He didn't like that we liked it, I think."

"He got through the film alright," I added. "It was just at the end he got annoyed when we started talking about it."

"Well, maybe I shouldn't watch it then. It might make me angry too," Isobel said. "This song is quite nice though."

Next it was Janis. Down On Me.

"So, let me ask you guys something," Isobel began, as if she was about to bring up something very serious. "Have you guys watched Breaking Bad?"

"Yes," said James.

"He watched it from the first episode," I said. "I only started watching it when it had nearly finished. I was sick of everyone talking about how great it was so I started watching it to catch up."

"Was it worth it?"

"Well …" I paused.

"Don't even try and say you didn't like it," James said.

"Are you about to kick off, James?" Isobel asked.

"I might. I won't sit here and listen to him badmouth Breaking Bad."

"I'm not going to badmouth it! I liked it. I did. It's good. It just … wasn't … the best thing ever."

Isobel was smiling. James was not.

"You're so contrary. Of course you'd say that. Everyone loves it so you can't."

"It's not that. It's just ... right, Isobel, have you ever seen The Wire?"

"For fucks sake ..." James said to himself.

"I haven't," Isobel said. "Should I?"

"Definitely. Now, what it is, and I know it's kind of a cliché to say it, but The Wire is the best T.V show I've ever seen. I wouldn't even know how you go about writing something like that. It's just so far beyond everything else I've ever seen that nothing else really compares."

"But Breaking Bad wasn't meant to be like The Wire. Not everything has to be The Wire," James said.

We'd had the same argument a few weeks before. It had been limited to texts. Now, in person, we could have it out in full.

"I know that. It's just ... Breaking Bad was good. Really good. It's really entertaining. It's definitely worth watching. It's just kind of ... normal," I said.

"Normal?!" James was not impressed.

"It's just like some other shows I've seen. I don't mean it's a rip off or anything. It's not. I don't know anything else similar. It's just a normal T.V show. I mean, it's one of the best. It's at the top of the pile. But it's still just a T.V show. It's not ..."

"The Wire."

"Exactly."

"Well, I didn't mean to get the two of you so riled up," Isobel said. "I was just wondering. All I know is it's about a teacher who starts making drugs. It didn't sound all that. People are always shocked I haven't seen it."

"I know it sounds kind of silly. Just trust me, it's worth it," James said. "The main character, he's just such a good character. You can't work out whether you're on his side or not. It's so tense the whole time. Even when they're sitting around having breakfast it's really gripping somehow. There's this guy in it, Jesse–"

"I liked Jesse," I admitted.

"–he's a drug addict and a bit of a twat sometimes," James continued. "But still, you end up rooting for him. It plays with you like that. You don't know what you want to happen. It's really good. You should definitely watch it."

"I think I might do. You've sold me on it," Isobel said.

The Doors were on. LA Woman.

"Thanks for putting this on by the way," I said.

"You're welcome. I mean, it's not like I put on a song just for you and you turned round and started an argument with me,"

"You're a good friend."

"You're damn right I am. It wasn't just for you though. I figured it was a good use of the money. It's like seven minutes long. We're getting our money's worth."

"Apart from compared to everywhere else in the world, where you don't have to pay to hear a song," Isobel said.

"Well, yeah, apart from anywhere else. In this exact situation though, I figured it was best to save us from that extra couple of minutes of awkward silence."

"Very wise," Isobel said.

Mr. Mojo Risin came and went. The Libertines. Don't

Look Back Into The Sun.

"I figured it made sense to end with this," James said.

"A fine choice," I said.

"I did make some fantastic choices," James repeated.

"Come on then, show us what you're made of," Isobel said, looking at me.

"What do you mean?"

"It's your turn. Go put something on. And hurry. We're only a few minutes away from silence. Nobody wants that."

"Fine."

I got up and went over to the jukebox. It was one of those modern ones where you type in the names. No vinyl in sight.

I saw James get up and head over to the bar again. He mouthed "coke?" at me and I gave him a thumbs up.

The song was nearly ending. I didn't have long.

I thought about when I first met Isobel. Izzy. Izzy Stradlin. She hadn't known the name. I thought it'd be a good thing to put on. Sweet Child. Guns N' Roses. I got there just in time. I knew the long solo in the middle gave me some breathing space before my next choice.

It was more difficult than I thought it would be. There were a few tabs on the screen that gave you suggestions. I flicked through and didn't find much that was useful. I waited for a moment of inspiration. Patti Smith. She never let me down. I thought about Because The Night. Didn't Springsteen write that too? I decided against it. Gloria. Perfect. The best version. Everybody knew it. That had the energy I was after. So what next? Hendrix seemed suitable. Ezy Ryder. I couldn't not choose it once I saw it. To hell with inspiration. The obvious choices were obvious for a reason.

The solo to Sweet Child kicked in.

I heard James, now back at the table, singing along with the guitar.

Done with imagination, the next choices came quickly. Stones again. Satisfaction. Sure. I typed Satisfaction in the track search box. The Stones came up first. Next to it was an Otis Redding version. I vaguely remembered hearing it somewhere before and liking it. I figured it was a slightly more interesting choice and went for it. I had one more choice to make then I was free.

Sweet Child was coming to a close. I thought about Otis Redding. I couldn't choose another one of his. I needed to pretend I had ideas. I'd always heard my mum listening to Otis Redding in the kitchen when I was a kid. Him, Sam Cooke and Ray Charles. That's what she always played while she cooked. I looked up Ray Charles. I Got A Woman. Short but perfect. We'd end up talking about Kanye West or the Ray Charles movie or something.

Patti Smith had started by the time I sat back at the table.

"I actually thought about putting Guns N' Roses on but decided against it. Great minds," James said.

"Do you remember when we first met? I told you about Izzy Stradlin in Guns N' Roses. You had no idea what I was on about," I said to Isobel.

"Yeah. Kind of," she said. "I don't mind not knowing stuff

like that. I like that song. I mean, everyone knows that song but it doesn't mean everyone knows the names of everyone who played on it."

"I know," I said. "I just store stuff like that in my brain. I mean, I don't even like Led Zeppelin that much but I still know all their names."

"They're different though," James said. "When they reunited more people applied for tickets than there are in the whole of the U.K. Or something crazy like that."

"I don't even want to think about how much those tickets cost," Isobel said.

"I know," I said. "I get angry when I have to pay a tenner to go to the cinema. I can't imagine paying a grand for a couple of hours of music."

"Ten pounds? It's only a fiver up here," Isobel said.

"That's because by the time films are on up here they've already been on T.V so there's no point going to the cinema," James said.

Gloria came and went and Hendrix kicked in.

"You know," James said "I'd complain about how predictable your choices were, but to be honest, I'm enjoying every one."

~~~~~

A few people came in. A couple of guys in suits and a woman in a smart skirt. They'd obviously just finished work.

"Intruders," Isobel said.

"It does kind of feel like that," I agreed.

They stood at the bar. The guy paying for the drinks tapped his credit card along to the music while he waited to pay. I felt validated.

"I never expect to see people in suits around here for some reason. I guess that's stupid really," James said.

"It's not that stupid. It's not like there's loads of office blocks around," Isobel said.

"Maybe they just dressed up because of all the great music they heard coming from the pub. Especially the last couple of songs," I said.

The newcomers sat at the opposite end of the pub to us.

"So, when are you guys off then?" Isobel asked.

"We're here tonight. Then we've got the party tomorrow night. Then we leave the morning after that," James said.

"The morning after? That'll be fun!" Isobel said.

"Yeah. I'm hoping this guy keeps up his no drinking thing just a couple more days. Then he can take the first driving shift that morning. At least it's only a little drive then we get a few hours sleep on the ferry."

"If it's running," Isobel said.

"What do you mean?" I asked.

"If the weather's shitty the ferry won't run," James said.

"Not just that," Isobel said. "It seems to break down every other week. I always hear people moaning about it. A couple of weeks ago, they found out the rudder was on the wrong way. Somehow. They had to send divers in underwater to try and sort it all out. That's what I got told anyway."

"On the wrong way? That's reassuring," I said.

"That wasn't the end of it though. They ended up sending this replacement ferry while it was getting fixed. It was this tiny little boat that usually goes to one of the smaller islands. It could only fit a few people on. It didn't have enough room for all the cars that had been booked on. They had to put people's cars on the freight ferry that brings over all the other stuff. It meant people got taken over to Ullapool and then had to wait around all day for their cars to get there."

"That's crazy," James said.

"Yeah, you'd think they'd have worked out a better back up plan," I said.

"One of the first things I got told when I got here was, never rely on the ferries. They always find new ways not to run."

"So yeah, I guess what I should have said was, we're meant to get the ferry Friday morning, but we might never leave," James said.

"Or we might leave Friday morning but our car might not leave until Friday night," I added.

"Exactly," Isobel said.

Otis Redding came on. Familiar riff. This time with horns.

"Who's this?" James asked.

"Otis Redding."

"Oh, yeah."

Some more people found their way in during Satisfaction. Four men. Three in jumpsuits. One had massive dirty patches over his knees. The difference in appearance between them and the last arrivals was huge.

"So, you're leaving Friday morning and you've still not been out to Tolstadh?" Isobel asked.

"I haven't. I will though. I'll do it tomorrow if the weather's good," I said.

"Forget that. Just go there anyway. You don't have to get out of the car for long. Just go there. You need to see a few different places. You can't just remember a few buildings and the castle and think you've been to Lewis," she said.

"She's right," James said.

"Promise me," Isobel said.

"I promise I'll try," I said.

"That's not good enough. Promise me."

"Fine. I'll go. I will. I'll go."

"Great."

Ray Charles had started.

"In the Kanye West version of this, how does it make sense that she's a gold-digger? It says she gives him money," James asked.

"I think he changed it round," I said.

"Oh, that makes sense."

Isobel hummed to herself.

"Yeah," she confirmed. "It's different in this one."

"This is my last song," I said. "Who's next?"

"I think we should get going actually," James said. "We've been here a while."

Isobel finished her glass. I did the same.

"No-one could top my choices anyway," I said.

"It does seem to be bringing the crowds in," James said.

A few more people had trickled in over the last couple of minutes. "Of course, it could just be the time of day when everyone is done with work."

"That seems unlikely," I said. "It's definitely the music."

"Do you want a lift up to yours?" James asked Isobel.

"If that's ok. I don't mind walking if it's out of the way for you guys," she said.

"Of course not. It literally adds about four seconds to our journey dropping you off."

"Well, I'll owe you four seconds then."

I took the empty glasses up to the bar. The woman thanked me. I thanked her. Then we left.

CHAPTER 28

I WASN'T REALLY KEEPING TRACK OF WHAT DAY OF THE WEEK IT WAS. Monday. Thursday. Saturday. It didn't really change anything. I just knew it was my last full day on the island.

James and I were on Rupert duty again. I didn't know what Rupert did with his days when we weren't with him. He seemed a pretty happy dog. His tail started going the second he saw James pick up the lead.

We went the same route as before. It seemed a long time ago. I remembered being kind of nervous about James bringing up anything too serious. Not now. I felt completely at ease.

James let Rupert off the lead. I watched his legs as he sprinted ahead of us. I watched his feet dart in and out of the shit on the floor. I looked up at the sky. It went on forever. I was going to miss the sky.

"What are you looking at?" James asked.

"Just the clouds," I said.

"Well don't. It makes you look mopey."

That brought me back. I didn't have anything to mope about. Leaving didn't have to be sad. Things coming to an end didn't mean anything sad. It was inevitable. Everything ends. It's a good thing. The Godfather would've been unbearable if it had never finished.

Rupert was darting around in front of us. He'd stop, dig his nose into any nearby crevice, then sprint ahead before suddenly stopping again at the next seemingly random spot.

"Does he remember where he's going?" I asked.

"Yeah. He gets taken out to the beaches and stuff too but he comes this way pretty much every day. He must know it by now."

"I wonder if he recognises all the smells. Like he can tell if someone new has been through here. That's why they piss on things right? To leave their smell? Does he just run from one spot to another thinking 'good, that's my piss' and then run on to the next spot?"

"Probably."

We both watched Rupert. He stopped, looked back as if he'd heard a noise, then carried on running. He pulled over to a patch of long grass. He sniffed. Then he set off again.

"All good there," James said.

"Good to know."

There were a couple of minutes of silence. I was thoughtlessly looking around, watching Rupert, when I realised I hadn't been speaking.

"Sorry. I just realised I've not been talking," I said.

"It's not like you've been ignoring me," James said. "Neither of us has said anything. You don't have to talk all the time you know."

~~~~~

Back at the house, Mary explained what was happening.

"Tomorrow's a holiday here. Everyone's got the day off. That's why we can have the party tonight. Usually we'd have it tomorrow but we'd much rather you two were here for it."

I felt a little out of place. I knew by 'you two' Mary had really meant her son. I just happened to be there. For the first time I felt like I was intruding.

"The thing is, there's some people we'd like to see," she said. "Older family, who probably won't want to stick around for the party when the house gets busy and everyone's drinking. So we've decided we'll have a bit of a lunch-dinner this afternoon and have the people over who won't be coming tonight. Then later everyone else will get here. Now Alex, of course you're welcome to have the meal with us, but I can't promise you'll enjoy it."

"Didn't you promise Isobel you'd go to Tolstadh today?" James offered helpfully.

"Yeah, I guess I did."

"Well, that's perfect then. You take the car over to Tolstadh and come back tonight for the party," Mary said.

"Let me guess-" James started.

"You're not going anywhere," Mary said.

"Great."

CHAPTER 29

IT WASN'T RAINING BUT THE WEATHER WASN'T GREAT. The giant skies and the grey weather left me in a bit of a daze as I drove.

I was surprised when someone tried to overtake me. It seemed unnecessary. That is until I got stuck behind a car crawling along at thirty miles an hour round bends that made it impossible for me to overtake. Then I got it. It was the island equivalent of walking down a street in London. Every time someone behind you gets angry because you've stopped in the street you wonder why they're so aggressive. Then when someone in front of you slows right down or stops unannounced you find it unbelievably frustrating.

I passed Stornoway and headed out in a direction I hadn't been yet. I'd seen Tolstadh on a couple of signs so I knew I was on the right track, for the time being at least.

Martin had tried to explain to me where to go. The route sounded straight forward enough. It was finding the beaches I was worried about. James said there were a few. A great long one, a smaller one and then another concealed one with some steep cliffs around. He promised me I couldn't miss them. But everyone always says that once they know where something is.

James told me it was about twenty minutes away. I knew the way his brain worked. I knew that meant it was at least twenty minutes away once I'd reached Stornoway. He had this weird way of breaking up time. At school he'd always done it. He'd say things like *it's only ten minutes until half past, then it's only two hours until the end of the day, so really it's only a few minutes until it's less than an hour from the last hour of the day.* I could usually just about follow what he meant but it didn't comfort me in the same way it did him.

I'd been on the same road for quite a while. I tuned into Island FM again. It was growing on me. It snapped me out of the mindlessness of the winding roads and everlasting scenery. My mind would wander during the repetitive squiggles of a fiddle and then Katy Perry would start one of her inane bouncy songs and it would bring me back again.

I started to feel like I was never going to see another town. I wasn't one hundred per cent sure which direction I was heading in. Not that it mattered whether I was heading North or East really, it just made the relentless forward motion feel kind of aimless.

The landscape was becoming more wild. I hadn't noticed any great hills in the road but I felt like I was climbing higher with each mile. Eventually I hit, in island terms, civilisation. I saw a small single-storey building with a post office sign out front. I slowed down. I noticed a brown sign. Brown meant tourist spots. It was pointing out the way to the coastal path. I thought about what Martin had said. I was pretty sure he'd told me to pass the sign rather than follow it. I decided to keep going. I figured I could always turn back if I needed. Of course, as James had taught me, turning back on island roads meant either driving for miles until you find a spot to reverse into, or waiting for the lanes to seem empty enough for you to spin round right in the middle of the road.

The road merged together into one small lane. The radio was singing to me in Gaelic. I turned the volume down. There was grass either side of the road. Martin had told me the best place to park was in the middle of some grass near a pond. I kept my eye out. I couldn't see any ponds. The grass disappeared and the landscape became wild again. It felt kind of prehistoric.

The bends were getting tighter. I slowed right down, turned the radio off. I couldn't see if a car was coming round the next corner so I couldn't afford to let my mind wander. I climbed a slope and met a tight left turn. As the car followed the road I found myself looking out the window to the right. The sea spread across the entire bottom half of the glass. The cloudy sky occupied the top half. That's all there was out there. Sea and sky. As I turned the corner I saw sand down to the right. It was a great long, clean stretch of beach. My eyes were already back on the road, but I knew what I'd seen. It was the long beach they'd told me about. In that instant I hadn't been able to take it all in. There was too much. I'd seen where it started but not where it ended. I wanted to see more. I wanted to be the one person down there. I decided I'd turn round at the next place I came across.

A minute or two later there was an opening at the side of

the road. I could see the top of a caravan about fifty metres away. I pulled off to turn round and head back towards the long beach. As I got near the caravan I realised I was in a gravelly sort of car park. Behind it was a sunken pond with a few birds sitting on the water. I saw a couple of rabbits speed off as I got close. I couldn't see the sea yet but I knew this was the spot Martin had described to me.

I parked far enough away from the caravan to not cause any disturbance. There was no sign of people outside and I didn't want to wake anyone if they were sleeping. Besides, I wasn't really in the mood for making small talk if anybody stuck their head out. I got out of the car quietly.

The land sloped down in front of me. It was sandy grass and piles of rabbit shit. I caught movement out of the corner of my eye and knew the rabbits must be running from me as I walked. It made me feel kind of guilty. I wanted to explain to them that they didn't need to panic. I saw a few holes in the ground. I wondered how many rabbits were down there, cowering, terrified about what I was going to do to them.

There was a small hill with a picnic bench on top. Only once I'd passed it did I see the beach below.

It wasn't that wide. I could see it all from where I stood. The beach dipped down between two hills either side. On the left a little river ran down and across the beach into the sea. On the right it was far more dramatic. There were tall stone towers standing out in the water. The sea had obviously found weak spots in the rock and worked its way in.

I followed the path of the stream onto the beach. It made

playful little noises as I walked. I thought about summer. I thought about kids growing up here with this just down the road. They probably didn't know how lucky they were. They probably spent every night wishing they had a McDonalds they could go to.

I felt strange. I'd been on beaches before, of course. That week I'd been on beaches just as clean, just as picturesque. I hadn't been on my own though. The one other time I'd been the only person on a beach I was twelve or thirteen. We were visiting my Gran down in Frinton. My mum and her were talking about something serious and told me to go out and walk around a bit. It was pretty late in the evening. I headed straight towards the beach. I didn't know anything else around there. It was absolutely freezing. There wasn't anyone about. The beach wasn't smooth. Wasn't clean. I had to watch my footsteps carefully. I couldn't focus on my thoughts. I had to dodge the rubbish left by the visitors who'd been there earlier in the day. Beer bottles. Burger packets. Half-eaten rolls. Stuff like that. I didn't feel any connection to the sea or the wind or the world. I just felt cold and lonely.

This was a completely different sensation. I felt like an intruder. A rightful intruder but an intruder all the same. I didn't feel like I shouldn't be there, I felt like I didn't deserve to be there. I couldn't understand how out of everyone on the planet I was the only one who got to be there.

I walked to the far side of the beach. There were smooth, black pieces of rock facing out to sea. The tall stone monuments in the water cast shadows back onto the beach. It was kind of intimidating. I tried to imagine the sea smashing into the land, only to meet these defiant towers standing tall, refusing to budge. I wondered if anyone had ever tried to climb them. The idea of standing on top of your own stone pillar was kind of satisfying.

I stood as close to the sea as I could without getting my shoes wet. One of the pillars straddled the line where the tide reached the sand. The sea had bore a hole right through the middle at the bottom. It had left a hollow cave just about big enough for me to stand in. I moved underneath the rock and felt the wind whipping through the small tunnel. I watched the tide come up to my feet then retreat back to sea. I made a mental note to ask James if he'd ever spotted it before. I wondered if you could sleep there. The wind would probably make it difficult.

The beach was kind of enclosed. The hills on each side made it feel like a private cove. I felt like the owners of the place could be standing on high, looking down, wondering what I was doing on their land. I turned and looked back across the beach. A single sheep was standing on the hill eating grass. He raised his head, looked at me, returned to his meal. It made me smile. He had no interest in the views or the isolation. He was just following his mouth until he ran out of grass. He was probably disappointed each time he hit a beach.

I decided to make a move for the car. The wind had put a chill through me and the beach wasn't quite big enough for me to keep moving. Besides, I knew that great long beach was waiting for me just a couple of minutes back.

As I walked back to the car the rabbits scattered across the grass again, back down into their holes.

CHAPTER 30

IT WAS A STEEP SLOPE DOWN TO THE TINY CAR PARK. I was the only car. There was a small stone building with a sign saying public toilets. It didn't look big enough to hold a single person.

The sand curved round the corner from the car park. The beach soon opened out in front of me and the wind hit. I leaned into it. I could just about make out the other end of the beach. I'd never seen one like it. When I was younger I'd been to Menorca with my mum. I remember one beach there seeming huge. It wasn't the same though. It was covered in a million tourists with all their towels and buckets and drinks. It felt artificial. There was more bare skin than bare sand. It was nothing like this.

I walked slowly. I didn't have anywhere to be. There wasn't anywhere else to be. My mind wandered while I walked. The sand was sturdy enough to not have to watch my steps. I wasn't used to just walking on my own. Especially without music. I tended to put headphones in wherever I went. Even at work, finding my way around the hospital, I'd pop in headphones just have something to distract me. Not now. As I walked I left shallow foot prints in the sand.

There was a lull in the wind. I stopped walking and faced out to sea. I lifted my hands up above my head and took a deep breath. I focused on the point where the sea met the sky. I imagined the water tipping over the horizon. I thought about work. I thought about my office. I thought about all that paperwork. I thought about the people there counting down to their days off. I thought about my old school. The kids worrying about things they'd forget a few years later. I thought about my mum. I wondered which direction she was in. I wondered if she knew how big the sea really was. I wondered if it'd help her if she knew. I thought about everything. There wasn't any pattern. The Royal Family. Amy Winehouse. Syria. Bob Dylan. George Carlin. X Factor. Westminster. Newsnight. Kerouac. Roald Dahl. Twitter. Wikileaks. Wimbledon. Wetherspoons. None of it was here. None of it could reach me here. On an empty beach with the endless sea nothing seems important. I felt a terrifying kind of peace. I couldn't find anything to worry about. I felt the breeze blow through me, clear me out. I felt small. Reassuringly small. Whatever I did the sea was still out there, crashing over itself. Nothing would change that. I closed my eyes. I tried to absorb it. I didn't want it to go. Sometimes I read a page of a book and find something worthwhile, something interesting, something inspiring. As the minutes pass I forget the exact wording, then the sentiment, then the author and eventually even the title of the book. I didn't want that to happen with this. I wanted it to stay. I wanted to trap it. Keep it. Bitterness always stuck around. Embarrassment lasted for years. Why not this? I willed it to stay, whatever it was.

I started walking again. My feet started sinking a little into the sand. I adjusted my path to walk slightly further from the water. The sand was sturdier there.

I thought about Isobel. I remembered her saying she loved to walk barefoot on the beach. I'd heard a few people say that before. I couldn't relate to it. The beach was giving me enough. I didn't need to freeze my feet to enjoy it more.

A couple appeared in the distance. There must've been another way onto the beach. I could see their dog running backwards and forwards. It was criss-crossing the sand in front of them. It would sprint down to the water then back up to the couple. Then it would sprint up to the grass, dig a little, then go back to check in with the couple again. It was a dark-coloured labrador. It soon spotted me. He darted straight at me. He jumped up and put his paws on my stomach. I put my hands behind his ears and gave him a scratch. His nose was muddy. His face was soaked. He looked like he was grinning.

"Hello," I said.

He panted, propping himself up against me.

The couple got closer. I couldn't quite make out their faces yet. I could hear the woman calling.

"Buckley! Down! Heel!" she shouted. Buckley took no notice of her.

"Buckley! Come back here!" she called again.

The dog slid down my front, leaving muddy stains on my stomach and thighs. He turned and ran back. I felt like it was more coincidental timing than any sign of obedience on his part.

The couple and I finally reached each other. They were younger than I expected. Mid-thirties at the latest.

"I'm so sorry," the woman said. "We don't usually let him off the lead. We thought the beach was empty."

"It's fine," I said.

The man was laughing. Buckley was now standing up against the man's stomach, his tongue dangling from his mouth in ecstasy.

"He's not aggressive, he just loves meeting people. He gets too excited," she said.

"Really, it's fine. I don't mind."

"Thank you. That's kind of you."

"No worries, have a nice evening."

"Cheers," the man said, "you too. Come on Buckley."

The couple began walking. Buckley sprinted off in front of them. I carried on walking in the direction they'd appeared from.

A few seconds later I heard a shout. It was the woman again.

"Buckley!"

I turned and saw Buckley hurtling towards me. This time I was ready. I crouched down. He jumped up. I caught him under his front legs. He put his paws on my shoulders. He looked me in the eyes. He tried to lick my face but I held him just out of reach. As nice as he was I didn't fancy having his saliva on my cheeks.

"Hello again, Buckley," I said, his body still wriggling excitedly in my arms.

"Buckley!" the woman called again.

"Time to go, Buckley," I said, letting his paws fall to the ground. I stood up and pointed back to his owners. He ran about twenty metres past me in the wrong direction, skidded in the sand, turned round and flew past me back towards the couple. I waved to the woman but she didn't see me.

I was reaching the far end of the beach. I was disappointed. The dog had distracted me, snapped me out of my happy daze. I touched the ground when I ran out of sand and turned round. It was like a relay. I remembered as a kid, running on sports day, missing the baton as a girl passed it to me. I instinctively started running anyway and had to go back to pick it up. I was embarrassed for ages after even though nobody else remembered it.

It was strange looking out at the sea. It was impossible to focus on just one spot. You keep your eyes fixed, you know where you're looking, right over there, just there, but the sea keeps going, keeps moving, writhing, pulsating into these different forms and patterns.

I felt an overwhelming sense of guilt. Guilt for all my moaning. Guilt for sitting around waiting for something to happen. Guilt at wasting opportunities. Guilt at not making the most of being alive. There were kids out there born without choices. Kids born without water. Without working legs. Without parents. Without caring parents. Without a calm bed to sleep in. Without anyone to play with. They never got the chance to change any of that. It was criminal for someone like me, with a comfy bed to sleep in whenever I needed, and a body to climb out of it whenever I wanted, to be so passive. I thought about being trapped in bed forever. There were days when I wished I could never get out of bed again. How laughable that was. How useless and petty. If I was truly stuck in bed forever, I'd do everything I could to affect my surroundings. I'd want my favourite books at the side of my bed. I'd want the walls a colour I liked, the sheets a kind I found relaxing. And here I was, not limited to one room, but with the whole world to play with, and I refused to make any decisions, any changes, and then had the nerve to moan about things when they didn't end up how I wanted.

It was ok to make wrong decisions. It was ok to not always choose wisely. The important thing was to choose, to grab. Once you become someone who makes decisions, who generates momentum, you can always turn again if you find yourself heading down the wrong path. Committing to something out of embarrassment, out of apathy or shame is ridiculous. Turning down a blind alley isn't stupid. It can happen to anyone. Endlessly sticking to it because you're afraid of how it looks when you're trying to find your way out – that's cowardice. If you find your own way out, on your own terms, it could end up a productive detour anyway. You might learn just what you needed to learn. There's no set route after all. No straight road. No one path.

The sea wouldn't be anywhere near as spectacular if it was one smooth single tide moving across the ocean bed. That's not how it is. There's a million variations. Each one bringing something new. A new momentum. A new shape. A new colour. A new trajectory.

The walk back felt shorter. Maybe I was more distracted. Maybe I walked quicker, wanting to get back to see everyone. Maybe it was just that I knew how long the beach was second time around. Things always seem to take longer when you aren't quite sure where they end.

I got back to the car sooner than I'd have liked. I thought about walking the whole beach again. I knew I'd get too cold and end up regretting it.

I sat in the car for a few minutes before I started the engine. I'd inhaled something powerful and wanted to gather myself. I didn't know if I'd ever come back to that beach again. I wasn't sure if I needed to.

~~~~~

I turned into Stornoway on the way back. I headed over to Tesco to pick up some flowers and a bottle of wine for Martin and Mary. I couldn't decide whether it was a thank-you or an anniversary present. I figured if I didn't get a card then they could take it either way.

Tesco was still pretty busy. There weren't too many flowers. I decided to go for the most colourful bunch I could find. I guessed which wine to get. I'd only ever bought wine based on the price. Never the cheapest. Always something on offer that made it nearly the cheapest. I figured that wasn't really the right sentiment for a gift so I ended up going for something expensive that was on sale at a cheaper-but-not-too-cheap price. It would have to do. I felt bad for not having thought of something more interesting to get them. I knew they wouldn't mind but they'd gone out of their way for me and I really wanted them to know how much I appreciated it.

At the house all the normal spots were taken. I had to back up the road a bit to find somewhere to leave the car. I ended up parking tight against a fence at the side of the road and hoping there was enough room for other cars to get past.

All the parked cars meant people had arrived. The idea of them all inside made me nervous. I always hated walking into a place on my own when people were already there. Of course, people don't really notice you when you walk into a shop, an office, a party. They just keep going with their conversations and their drinks and whatever else it is they're doing. It never feels like that though. I always feel like deep down they're all thinking about me, judging me.

I'd felt anonymous back on the beach. In a peaceful, reassuring way. I took a deep breath and tried to draw some of that back. It had given me an enthusiasm. A spark of life I'd been missing or at least hiding from. I needed to carry that with me. It was stupid to feel nervous. It was natural too, I couldn't stop it. But it didn't have to be the only thing I felt. I wasn't only nervous. I was excited as well. I wanted to thank Martin and Mary. I wanted to make sure they had a good night. I wanted to see what James had been up to. I wanted to tell Isobel I'd finally made it over to Tolstadh.

CHAPTER 31

I WALKED INTO THE KITCHEN. There was a guy I didn't recognise pouring himself a glass of wine from one of the many bottles on the table. He turned as I came in.

"Mary's just through there," he said.

I thanked him. I had no idea if I'd met him before. He might've just seen the flowers and known they'd be for Mary.

I met Mary in the hall. She was stroking Rupert and telling a story about when he was a puppy. I let her reach the punchline – a tiny Rupert leaping up, pulling a cake down off the kitchen counter and eating it all. She was a good storyteller. It wasn't a particularly funny story but she told it with such warmth and enthusiasm that it was hard not to get caught up in it. As the laughter settled, she turned and saw me standing there.

"Those better not be for me," she said.

"Not just you," I said.

"Well, I'm sure Martin will love the flowers. So I'm guessing this is my present?" she said, reaching for the bottle of wine. I told her I trusted her to see it got where it needed to go.

"She has no problem finding room for wine!" a woman I

didn't know said, as if she'd just uttered the most outrageous thing in the world.

Mary gave me a big, flowery hug and went off to find somewhere to leave them. I crouched down and scratched behind Rupert's ears. He tried to lick my face. I let him get as near as possible without actually touching me. I didn't want to seem ungrateful, but I'd just had a near miss with Buckley and I didn't want to spend the night stinking of Rupert's tongue either.

"How come you never greet me like that?"

I looked up. It was James.

"Because when you try to lick my face it's impossible to hold you back," I said.

"The heart wants what it wants."

He had a bottle of beer in his hand. Nearly empty. I guessed it wasn't the first.

"How's today been?" I asked.

"Oh, a laugh riot," he said.

"I bet."

"I mean, it was fine. It was nice. Mum had a good time I think. Oh! That reminds me. I met this guy today. Let's go find him. Come on dear."

He took me by the hand and started walking. When I wriggled my hand free he grabbed it again even tighter. We headed through to where the dining table was. There were a bunch of people sitting around. Too many for the room really. Some were sharing chairs. Others had found make-shift stools.

"Mike," James said.

There were a couple of guys standing up against the wall. They both turned.

"This is Alex, my mate who's up with me," James said.

Mike reached out and shook my hand.

"Ask Mike what he does," James said to me.

"So Mike, what do you do?"

"I work at the council," Mike said.

"No! You know what I mean, tell him what you were telling me earlier," James said.

Mike looked embarrassed.

"I was just telling James here about some of the stuff you can do round here. Last weekend we went rock-climbing over on the west side."

"Rock climbing!" James said, hitting me on the arm.

"Is that scary?" I asked.

"It looks worse than it is. You don't do stuff you're not certain that you're safe doing. Or at least as safe as you can be in those situations."

"I don't know if I'm brave enough to do anything like that," I said.

"It's not bravery," Mike said. "It's just like anything. First time you do it you're nervous. I remember the first time I went fishing I was worried about it because I didn't know what I was doing. It's not like anything bad could happen but I still worried. This is just like that. Anything new seems tricky. You get better the more you do it."

He spoke with a genuine modesty that only made him more impressive.

"I'm not much of a swimmer though, so if I was fishing on a boat I would have something to worry about," I said.

"It's not like we're trying to wrestle sharks out of the water. You'd be fine," Mike said.

"We went out on Martin's boat the other day actually. It was really cool. You just turn the corner out the back and suddenly it feels like you're out in the middle of nowhere."

"I completely forgot about your swimming when we did that," James said.

"I did think you were being surprisingly restrained. You didn't pretend to push me in once."

"If I'd have remembered I'd have made the boat rock about a bit more."

"I believe you," I said.

Mike laughed.

"Oh! Ask Mike what club he runs!"

Mike smiled his embarrassed smile.

"So, Mike, what club do you run?" I asked.

"I was telling James earlier how in the summer I run the scuba club here. It's only a few of us," he explained. "We go out diving together. It's not really a club. I'd just been talking to a couple of guys at canoe club and it turned out we were all into it."

"Canoe club too?" I asked.

"Oh, I don't run that. There's a bunch of people. Most of them are much better than me. It's cool though. We go out on these trips every now and then, down in Harris. We take our kayaks out and bring dinner for everyone."

"That's cool," I said. "I never really expected stuff like that here. It doesn't fit in with what the islands are like in my head."

"Yeah," Mike said. "Everyone thinks of it as this really peaceful place even though they know there's great mountains and water around. Nobody ever puts together that you can do this sort of stuff up here. It's one of the best places in Europe if you're into it."

"I feel like I need to come back up again and try the islands your way," I said.

"Do it! Next time you're up give me a call. I'd happily take you guys out," Mike said.

"You say that now Mike, wait until next year when you get the call," James said. "You'll hardly remember who we are and you'll take us out and we'll be shit at everything. We'll get it all wrong. Then you'll regret it."

"Well, I'm hoping you won't be a few beers down if we go out rock climbing," Mike said.

"I can't promise anything," James said.

Meeting Mike surprised me. If I'd been down South, I never would've imagined bumping into anyone like him on the island. I guess I had this apathetic arrogance. Other places are different. The people there must be different too. Not interesting different. Dull different. Not worth thinking about.

James had finished his drink. He demanded we go find him another so we made our way back through to the kitchen.

He was surveying the bottles out on the table when Isobel came through the door.

"I'm not late am I?" she asked.

"We've been worried sick!" James said.

"How are you?" I asked her.

"Not too bad, thank you. More importantly, what have you done today?"

"Well, I went to Tolstadh if that's what you mean."

"Did you crawl there?" she asked, looking at Buckley's stains on my trousers.

"No, I drove thanks."

"So, Tolstadh. Nice, isn't it?" she said.

"Yeah. It really was. I went to both beaches. The long one and the one with those big rock bits standing in the sea."

"That's a great story Alex," James said. "You should turn that into a book. The time you saw those big rock bits."

"James!" Mary called. "Come through here a minute."

James picked up a bottle of wine and sighed.

"I'll just keep this with me," he said, walking out.

"I'm glad you made it over to the beach. It would've been a shame if you'd left without seeing it," Isobel said.

"Yeah, I loved it. I was really at ease there. I feel like I was on the verge of working something out but I can't quite remember what it was now."

Isobel laughed. "I know what you mean," she said. "I always get that when I go for long walks on my own."

"Can I offer you a drink?" I asked, gesturing towards the table of bottles.

"I've got one here, thank you."

She reached into her bag and pulled out a bottle.

"I found one of these in my bedroom. I don't even remember buying it. I really like these sweet ciders but they do taste like kids drinks. Which is actually a bit dangerous really."

"Because kids might drink them?" I asked.

Isobel pulled a face.

"I meant because you drink them really quickly and don't realise how much you've drunk."

"That does make more sense," I admitted.

A roar of drunken laughter came from somewhere in the house.

"Sounds like I've got some catching up to do," Isobel said.

"Yeah, I was just thinking you weren't being loud and obnoxious enough."

"It's not too bad outside at the minute actually. Let's go out for a bit," she said.

I didn't protest. We headed out the way she'd just come in.

CHAPTER 32

I FINALLY GOT TO SIT ON THAT BENCH IN THE GARDEN, THE ONE LOOKING OUT OVER THE WATER. It was just dark enough to mean you couldn't really make out the water's edge. You just got the odd flicker of movement as the shallow light bounced off the gentle waves.

"So, when is it you guys actually leave? I know you told me," Isobel said.

"Tomorrow morning. I think the ferry's pretty early. I'm trying not to think about it."

"At least you won't be hungover."

"I don't just mean the morning. I mean leaving in general. I'm not excited about it."

"It is nice here," Isobel said.

"It's not just that. I'm not looking forward to going back. You know, back to normal life."

"Why not?"

"It's just … I don't know. Work. I don't really like work. At all. It's not terrible or anything it's just kind of soul-destroying. I'm still living with my mum. I was trying to save up for … something. I just … don't know. I don't really know what I'm going to do."

"That's not a bad thing."

"I guess not. It's just … I don't think I'm brave enough to change the things I don't like. I know I'll just slip back into it. I made one big decision once and committed so much to it and it ended up being totally the wrong decision. I ended up over-committing to try and save it. I think that's what I was thinking about at the beach. How easy it is to get dragged down by these stupid mistakes."

"Look, I know we've not known each other that long, but I like you. I can tell you're not stupid." She sipped from her bottle. "Listen. Let me tell you something. I try not to bring it up too much because I don't like to think I still live in context of it, but I think you'll get what I mean. When I finished my degree, I moved in with my boyfriend at the time. We hadn't lived together at uni. We spent every night together anyway, we just didn't think we were ready to move in together properly yet. Then, when I graduated, we both found jobs and we got a flat. One night he'd been out with some people from work. He came in drunk and was being really weird. At uni we'd not really drunk together much. We'd go out with our own friends to drink so I hadn't seen him drunk that many times before. So, he comes in really drunk and I don't like it. I tell him he should go to bed and sleep it off. He gets really angry. He grabs me and yells at me. He tells me never to fucking tell him what to do. It was scary. Really scary. It's not something I like to admit but, you know, he was a big guy, I'm only small, if he wanted to hurt me there's nothing I could do about it. The next day he didn't even mention it. He was hungover all day. I figured maybe he didn't remember. It seemed pretty out of character so I tried to forget it too. A few weeks later the same thing happens. Goes out after work. Comes in drunk. Starts yelling at me. Nothing physical really. When he got to bed he fell asleep straight away so I slept in the living room. I was pretty shaken up by it. It happened a couple more times before I even really acknowledged it was happening. One time he grabbed me by the face. He was yelling at me telling me I wasn't listening to him. I felt so bad. It wasn't happening that often but it made me feel like shit all the time. I was so embarrassed. I felt like I had to try and work out a way to deal with it. I didn't want to have to tell anyone. I'd chosen where to live based on this guy. I couldn't think about leaving him. My whole life revolved around him. My job, my house, everything. One time when he went out after work I decided to go out too. I went to this Starbucks near where we lived. I'm not usually fussed about places like that but I knew the one near us stayed open pretty late. I sat drinking coffee and reading the paper. I had my phone with me and I rang a couple of people I hadn't spoken to in a while just to chat. I even ended up reading the weird local paper with those little nothing news stories. Anything to keep me occupied. It got kind of late and the place was closing. I knew it wasn't late enough. I knew he wouldn't be home yet. I didn't want to be there when he got in. I decided to walk around. I just walked. I walked round town and then out of town and then back in again. It was dark so I followed wherever the streetlights led me. Eventually I realised I'd have to go home at some point. I couldn't walk all night. I knew he'd be angry when he got in and I wasn't there. I knew he'd be angry whatever I did. Then I got this text from a friend of mine. It was a normal drunk text. Telling me how much she loved me or something. Lots of exclamation marks. I decided to ring her. I asked her what she was doing. She told me she'd just got in from some bar somewhere. My brain did something. It clicked. I didn't think. I asked her if I could come over. She was drunk, you know, she would've said yes to anything. So that was it. I got a taxi. It cost like a hundred and fifty quid. The second I got in the taxi all that tension and worry drained out of me. I felt free from it. I'd solved the problem by doing something. Anything. It wasn't my problem anymore. It wasn't something I had to deal with. I don't mean that running away solves things, it doesn't. I wasn't running away. I was finally taking charge of myself. I decided where I was going. I decided what I was doing. I was going to see someone I liked. That was it. I turned my phone off once I got there. We stayed up all night talking. Not anything serious. Just silly catch up talk. The next day she drove me back to the flat. She waited outside in the car. I went inside and told him I was moving. I didn't let him drag it out. I didn't let him make an argument out of it. He was hungover which probably helped. I didn't try and make him feel bad either. I didn't want it to be about him. It was my choice. My decision. A few days later we got all my stuff and I moved back home for a bit. I didn't want to be anywhere which reminded me of all that. I knew I couldn't stay in my job anymore. Everything reeked of him. I ended up getting one of those jobs in South Korea. You know, teach English as a foreign language? I did that for about a year. Nobody knew who I was. Everything that happened was completely down to me. I'd have to walk into a room of people I didn't know, who didn't speak my language, and try and get my point across. I think that really helped. It gave me confidence. Some of it was crappy. Sometimes the hours were really long and you didn't get paid much at all. But it was ok. I'd made a choice for me and I knew if it didn't work out I could make another choice. Does that make sense?"

"Making your own choices? Yeah, I think so. Yeah. Definitely."

It was re-assuring to look at someone like her and think she'd felt as pathetic as I did. More so even. She'd felt trapped and embarrassed. It was crazy to think about. She walked so well. She oozed a subtle kind of confidence. She wasn't arrogant or anything. She was just so completely herself and seemed to exist outside of everything else going on around her. It seemed impossible to me that anything had punctured her the way she'd described.

I'd been carrying what had happened around inside me like a great iceberg in my chest. It chilled me and I couldn't do anything about it. I didn't like to shake it up for fear it would move against the inside of my ribs and freeze me stiff. It had filled me up completely. There was no room for anything inside me except this great, heavy absence. It kept me still. It weighed me down. I thought about the story Isobel had just told. She didn't have any self-pity in her voice. She was telling the story as it happened. She wasn't denying the reality of it.

Nor was she crushed by it. It's just how it was. Her energy had melted it. It was in these small manageable chunks she could pour out whenever she wished. It was still a part of her, but she was in charge of it. She'd made room for other things now. Lots of other things. Better things. More important things that wore away at that chill inside her. There didn't seem to be much of it left anymore.

"The thing is," I said, "I worry that it's easy for me to talk about. It's easy for me to say 'I'm moving on!' and pretend I'm feeling defiant. I just worry that when I'm back on my own I'll feel all shitty again and not do anything about it."

"Of course. That's part of being human. Your emotions are never going to be rational. Sometimes you'll feel sad for no reason. You can't control that. You've just got to work out which emotions to believe in. Which to put your stock in. If you know it's not worth being sad, if you know you can do something about it, then you've got to try and invest in the doing something."

"I know that. I do know all that. The thing is, since I've been up here, I've kind of forgotten about it all. I've felt good. Really good. For the first time in ages. I've not worried about anything really. I feel like you can do anything here. There's no pressure on you. There's just so much space. It gives you time to get used to yourself."

"Yeah. That's true. It's something I like about being here," she said.

"But then, I feel like I've just taken a holiday from real life. Once I'm back everything goes back exactly how it was before.

I won't know what to do when I go back to feeling the same way again."

"What you've got to remember is, the you up here, the you talking to me now, that's the same person who is going back to the mainland. Just because something didn't work out how you expected doesn't mean your life is any less fulfilling. Unless you decide it's going to be. This is how I think about it; I know it sounds stupid-"

She paused, looked me in the eyes, looked down at her bottle, scratched the label a little and then carried on talking.

"-so don't worry if it doesn't make much sense. I've not really thought about this out loud before. I just really want you to understand. It's something like this. Now, if you're really good at maths and this isn't right, let me get to the end before you tell me how wrong I am. So. There are an infinite number of numbers, right? You can't run out of numbers. You can keep counting forever. There's no end to it. Now, if that's the case, then that means there must be an infinite number of even numbers too. If you only counted even numbers you could still do it forever without running out. So, in a way, there are the same amount of even numbers as there are numbers in total. I just think about life like that. There are an infinite amount of things you can do. There are always choices. Always options. You never know what's going to happen. Someone might walk into your life and leave with all the odd numbers. That doesn't mean you've got any less possibilities. You've still got an infinite number of even numbers to play with. You've still got as many opportunities as you always did."

Then she stopped. She looked up to check whether I was still following her. I didn't speak for a second or two, so she did.

"Sorry. I know that doesn't make any sense. I think all the sugar in this made my mouth a bit hyper."

"It definitely makes sense. I was thinking about this earlier at Tolstadh. It's like, if you were stuck in bed all day, you'd do what you could to get the bedsheets you like, the walls a colour you like …"

"Exactly!" she said.

"Yeah, so don't worry. That definitely made sense. You're right. I completely get it. It's just like, I've spent so many years of my life staring at one person in one room that I didn't even care whether I was happy doing it or not. Then when the person left, suddenly the room looked empty. All I had was this empty room. I completely forgot that I could leave the room. That there's a whole world and billions of people just outside the door. It's just a case of…being brave enough to turn around and step outside."

"I think that makes more sense than what I said."

"Not at all. Everyone knows what I just said. Everyone knows that you've got to get over stuff. But that doesn't help them do it. What you said…it's like a reason why they should do it. Not just to avoid being sad but because it's exciting and means anything can happen and you can do anything. It's like, it's easy to feel a kind of shame when things don't work out how you expect. But what you said, it's something that trumps that. If you get caught up feeling sorry for yourself then you ignore all the great things you could be doing instead."

"I'm really glad you got that," Isobel said. "I got about half way through and had no idea where I was going with it."

"Well, you winged it pretty well."

"And remember, don't worry tomorrow if you still feel bad about leaving. You should. It's great here."

"Oh, thanks. That whole big speech and now you're telling me I should feel bad in the morning."

"Yeah. I'm thinking of becoming a motivational speaker."

"Makes sense," I said. "Motivate people then demotivate them straight away. That way they have to come back."

"Exactly. It's just good business."

~~~~~

We were back inside. Mary was telling stories about when James was little. Everyone was laughing. James was taking it well. At one point he got his own back, telling a story about the time Mary had come back late at night from a friend's house and proceeded to try and do the washing up loud and drunk in the kitchen.

James turned to Isobel. "So, do you think you'll still be here when I'm back up next year?"

"I don't know. Maybe. I'm not really planning that far ahead. What's that line? God laughs when he hears you make plans. Something like that."

"Yeah but it was John Lennon who said that. And he

thought he was a walrus. Don't take his word on anything."

"Either way, I like it here. I'll stay until I have somewhere better to move to," Isobel said.

"That's a pretty good situation to be in," James said.

"And you?" Isobel said, turning to me. "Will you be coming back with James next time?"

"If they'll have me again, I reckon so. I want to see more of the islands. I've still not seen most of Harris."

"That's what I was going to say. I'll do you a deal. If we're both here next year, I'll take you down to Harris and–"

"–deal!" I said.

"I wasn't finished," Isobel said. "I'll take you down to Harris, on one condition. That you've done something you feel good about by then. I don't know what. It's not up to me. I'm not telling you what to do. But you've been telling me how unhappy you are and I'm not going to listen to you make all the same complaints again next year."

She was smiling.

"Fair enough," I said.

"Hallelujah!" said James.

CHAPTER 33

I WAS STILL PRETTY TIRED WHEN I GOT UP. I'd set an alarm on my phone but I didn't need it. I was so worried about oversleeping that I ended up checking the time every half hour through the night.

The shower helped a little bit. Breakfast a little bit more.

Mary was up before me. She was down in the kitchen making bacon. She called up to James. There was no answer.

"Go get him, will you?" she instructed more than asked.

I went back upstairs. James was snoring his alcohol snore. I said his name a couple of times. Still no response. I put my foot on his forehead. He rolled over, eyes still closed. I said his name once more. Then I crouched down over him. He opened his eyes. Just.

"What?"

"We've got to go soon. Your mum's making breakfast."

"That woman."

Once he'd started eating, James perked up a bit.

"I feel pretty awake now," he said.

"That'll pass," I said.

"No, really, I do," he assured me.

"You always say that the morning after drinking, then by lunch you crash again."

"That doesn't sound like me. Maybe just to be safe though, how about I drive us to the ferry? Then you take the first stretch on the mainland. Just in case I get sleepy."

"Yeah, that's fine" I said. "That's what I'd assumed was happening."

CHAPTER 34

JAMES FELL ASLEEP BEFORE THE FERRY HAD EVEN STARTED MOVING. It was morning and the papers hadn't been brought on board yet. I wasn't sure what to do with myself. I remembered the books in my bag.

Sitting down I couldn't really feel the ferry rocking. The people walking past me had a bit more trouble. They'd cling to the handrail at the side and weave across the floor as the motion of the boat knocked them off course. It made it difficult to focus on reading. I'd catch them stumbling on the edge of my vision and couldn't help but put the book down each time and watch.

I knew I had at least a few hours of driving waiting for me. I looked at James slumped across his seat. He didn't look like he'd ever be capable of driving a car again. I got a bottle of water and a coke.

I watched the mainland appear through the window. There were patches of houses scattered across the hills. There were probably more people watching those houses through the ferry window than there were living in them. I thought about what it'd be like to live in one of those houses. I still wasn't sure if it appealed or not.

Ullapool. I recognised it once we got near. It was a pretty unique looking place. I woke James up and told him we'd be there in a few minutes.

"Give me a few more minutes, then," he said, eyes firmly shut.

Once we'd stopped I woke James again.

"Five more minutes," he said.

"We're here now," I told him. "They've opened the doors down to the deck. You can have five more minutes but I can't promise I or the car will be here when you get up."

That won him over. Just.

We were one of the first cars to be let off. I got a big playlist up on my phone while I waited for the signal. I put it on shuffle so that I didn't have to choose while I was driving. I knew I couldn't rely on James to stay awake and do it for me.

Within a couple of minutes we were out of Ullapool. We were off. The long road back. The mountains ahead of us had snow covered tops. It was hard to tell where they ended and the cloudy sky began.

James had his feet up on the dashboard. His head was resting on his seatbelt. I thought he was sleeping. It surprised me when he spoke.

"When are you back at work?" he asked.

"Monday."

"At least you get a bit of rest before."

"Yeah, I guess," I said. "To be honest, I'm thinking about handing in my notice."

"About time. What do you reckon you'll do instead?"

"I've no idea."

"Fair enough," he said.

I pressed for the next track. The Hold Steady. Stuck Between Stations. Great song.

ACKNOWLEDGEMENTS

I am endlessly grateful for the following people:

Callum and Orla Urquhart, Sarah Gerrard, Andy Yearley, Catherine Byrne and Jaya – for being the best friends anyone could ever ask to share an island with.

Mum, Dad and Keira – for being so understanding.

Sandy Barr, Todd Gilbert, Remy Maguire and Luke Sharpin – for their never-ending friendship and occasionally sensible advice.

Tom Buckenham, James Lamming and Tom Spraggs – for supporting and humouring me all this time.

James Bugg, Frankie Clough and Pete Whitmell – for making room in their lives for such a gigantic ego.

Sasha Davies and Stu Ponsford – for being such cool dudes.

Amanda Jenkins – for her selflessness and attention to detail.

Matthew at Urbane – for all his hard work and support.

Faye Savory – for everything.

http://www.jaredacarnie.com

@jacarnie

Jared A. Carnie is originally from Essex. He has since lived in Bath, the Outer Hebrides and Sheffield.

His writing frequently appears in various journals, zines and anthologies. He has read at numerous events and festivals and was awarded a New North Poets Award at the Northern Writers Awards 2015.

Waves is his debut novel.

Urbane Publications is dedicated to developing new author voices, and publishing fiction and non-fiction that challenges, thrills and fascinates.

From page-turning novels to innovative reference books, our goal is to publish what YOU want to read.

Find out more at

urbanepublications.com